UNDER HIS SHEETS

ACCIDENTALLY UNDERCOVER

R.L. MERRILL

Published By: Celie Bay Publications LLC
Edited By: Kelli Collins – Edit Me This
Cover Design: Covers By Jo

Part of the Accidentally Undercover Series

 Created with Vellum

A NOTE ABOUT LANGUAGE

Before you dig into the story, I want to explain a little about the use of different languages in this book.

Folks who live in Catalonia speak Catalan. They also speak Spanish, and most speak English. On my 2018 visit to Barcelona, I noticed that the Catalan people spoke a combination of all three, which made things extra spicy for me trying to practice my Castellano, the language we here in the U.S. refer to as Spanish, which is very different from the Spanish that most Americans speak. Phew! If you're confused, please keep reading.

Our hero Alonso not only speaks English, Catalan, and Spanish, but he was stationed in Italy for part of his military service and learned to speak Italian. Don't worry, I didn't add any Italian into this book, but there is a little French. More on that later. I wanted to try to reflect the way a true Catalan man would speak to his American lover. To prepare to write the dialogue, I watched TV shows set in Barcelona, countless videos on YouTube, read articles in The Local and other Spanish news sites, and started learning beginning Catalan on Duolingo—you have to be a fluent Spanish speaker, which I am not, so it turned out to be a review for my Spanish as well—and to be sure I did a decent job, I asked my trusty narrator friend Carlos to give the book a read.

Carlos is such a great sport. He returned the book with loads of lessons about using Catalan and Castellano as well as corrections to my accents (I SUCK at using accent marks) and suggestions for better phrases to use. He also called me out on my "Mexican Spanish" (hola, California girl here!), though I'm sure this will continue to be an issue for me moving forward, especially if I never get to live my dream of an extended trip to Spain. I am so grateful for his work on the book.

All of this is to say that Catalan and Spanish are alike yet very different, and confusing as heck. For example, In English, the word Catalan should be without the accent, and the first letter in caps. In Spanish, it's catalán. In Catalan, it's català. You can imagine my level of... perplexment? Perplexivity? Perplexion? Perplexity! Anyway, it's a lot. Therefore, I made some stylistic choices. You'll notice a few other differences: señor/a vs. the Catalan senyor/a, or the spelling of Catalonia vs Catalunya, and the different spellings for gracias vs. gràcies. I do go back and forth, but I try to use the correct spelling for whichever language is native to the current speaker. Bear with me. I hope it is not too distracting. Most importantly, I want you to swoon over Randall and Alonso, and hopefully be entertained by the hijinks they find themselves involved in.

To Alli and Layla
Thanks for letting me come along on this mission with you, Cari,
Linden, and M.A.
I've got your six.

ONE

NOVEMBER 13, 2019
10:53 PM Las Ramblas, Barcelona, Catalonia, Spain

All crowds were not created equal, nor did they evoke the same sensations.

Standing shoulder to shoulder with thousands of music fans at the rail on a rainy day in Nuremburg at Rock am Ring after playing a wild set with my band, MoonCraft, was one of my favorite experiences.

Standing back to front on Las Ramblas in Barcelona, with hundreds of protestors shouting in Catalan their desire for independence from Spain and justice for the separatists while police barricaded the side streets, not allowing anyone in or out of the protest, getting shoved and stepped on in the sweltering late-summer heat, wasn't likely to rank in my top ten of anything other than terrifying.

"Por favor. Soy americano," I shouted to one of the officers dressed in riot gear. "No quiero estar aqui." I thought that was the right way to tell him I didn't belong anywhere near this damn protest. I just wanted to get to a bar and lose my worries in a bottle of something strong enough to wash away the stench of what my life had become in the last two weeks since we'd come to Catalonia.

The cop pushed me back into the crowd of protestors who were waving yellow flags with red stripes and a blue triangle with a white star and into...

A frowning Spaniard with short, curly hair, long sideburns, a hard body, and a deep chin dimple covered in dark stubble.

"Cuidado."

"Lo siento," I said before another wave in the crowd pushed me into him again. I lost my balance and was about to go down when he caught me under the arm.

"Ves amb compte."

"I'm sorry."

My English must have startled him because he pulled me back in close and his eyes widened in surprise.

"You're the American."

Not *an* American, but *the* American? And he wasn't asking. When I kept gaping like a fish out of water, he adjusted his grip and yanked me forward, somehow making the crowd part for us. I tripped more than once as he dragged me through the chanting crowd that was yelling "independencia," and I ended up draped over his back as he dragged me toward the barricades on the far side of the corridor. He said something to the cop, who moved aside just enough for my savior to slip through with me in tow.

"Where are we..." I started to ask when he stopped to punch in a code in an alcove of a building a block or so off of Las Ramblas.

"You'll be safe inside."

"Thanks, but I was just trying to get to a bar—"

"I have drinks upstairs."

He led me up three flights and down a dark hallway to an

apartment door. Another keypad dealt with and he opened the door, moving inside quietly and disappearing into the darkness.

Should I follow? The last time I'd followed a stranger into a dark, unfamiliar apartment... Okay I'd never done this before. You'd think as a musician who'd been touring the world with his band for the past four years, I'd have had wild, adventurous experiences like that. If you did, well, you'd be sorely disappointed.

"Ven aquí, guiri."

"Excuse me?" I asked. "What did you call me?"

I walked down the entry hallway into the apartment and into the dimly lit living room with sparse furniture and no decor to speak of. Not even a wall calendar or a plant.

The man stood in front of a large window, which overlooked the chaos we were just in. The lights from police vehicles bounced off the bare walls, giving a red hue to the place.

"¿Hablas inglés?"

"Yes, I do, better than you speak Spanish." His words were soft though, so I didn't take offense.

"Thank you for getting me out of there," I said, looking down into the crowd. It was much denser than I'd thought and went on as far as I could see. "I shouldn't impose."

"You're Randall, right? From that band MoonCraft?"

That was the last thing I thought he'd say. "I was. We broke up. Now I'm just Randall."

"Why break up? You were good."

"Have you seen us?"

He nodded. "I have. At Sala Razzmatazz. It was a good show." He opened a bottle of wine and poured two glasses. "I loved the cover you did of that Mike Patton song, 'Deep Down.' Wasn't expecting that." He handed me a glass and when I paused, he gestured to it. "I said I had drinks. You look like you could use one."

"Thanks." I accepted the glass and pushed all thoughts of stranger danger out of my head. "Yeah that Mike Patton stuff is a vibe." And super niche. How did this guy know the album *Mondo Cane?*

He nodded once and turned his gaze back to the street below the window. There was surprisingly little noise from the protest inside his apartment, and though it had been a sultry night outside, it was cool, probably due to the ceiling fans.

"It is lucky I saw you. You could have been arrested. Being American might have made things difficult for you."

"Losing my passport would do that too." I finished my wine and without missing a beat, he refilled it.

"How did you manage that?"

"The same reason my band broke up. We got robbed two weeks ago, right after that show that you saw. All of our gear? Gone. Most of my personal stuff gone. That was the last straw. We were on our last few Euros we'd budgeted for the tour and couldn't play the rest of the gigs we'd booked without buying all new instruments and equipment, so the guys decided to bail. I've been sitting around my hotel waiting for my appointment at the embassy, trying to figure out my next move. It was not my plan to get involved with a protest, I was just looking for a bar to spend my last night in Spain, potentially, before my appointment tomorrow. Then I can go home, not that I'm looking forward to that."

Last sip. He refilled. I didn't know why I was unloading my tale of woe on him, but he was the first person I'd spoken to in a couple of days and he carried himself like someone who...cared. I still wasn't sure why he'd brought me to his home, though. No red flags had jumped out, but I was still a bit...confused.

"I suppose I was in the right place at the right time, then. Can't have you being detained. Though it's too bad you're leaving."

I was halfway through my third glass of what was exceptional wine when his words struck me. "Why's that?" It almost sounded like he was flirting?

He moved my way with the bottle, filling my glass before I could finish.

He shrugged. "Seems a shame for you to leave España on a low note."

For the first time, he made prolonged eye contact with me, and while I wouldn't call it a smile, there was definitely humor in the curve of his lips, his dark red lips that cut dramatically into his olive skin. His short, dark brown, curly hair was lightly sprinkled with gray, making it tough to tell how old he was. Maybe he was prematurely gray? But I felt like, the way he carried himself, he was older than my twenty-seven years old. But not like *old* old.

The weight of the past two weeks seemed to dissipate as I looked at this incredible specimen of Spanish finery. He wasn't much taller than me, maybe 5'10", but the way he filled a pair of jeans made me want to weep, and when I'd been draped over his back, I'd felt his powerful grip, his exceptionally large deltoids, and he hadn't faltered under my weight, which wasn't insubstantial.

I'd been told I had a pretty face, pretty hair, and a stunning voice, but I certainly wasn't built like most rangy, lanky singers in rock bands. My DNA meant no matter what I tried, I always carried extra padding around the middle and my ass *really* didn't quit. It hadn't mattered to me much until MoonCraft fell prey to the number two band killer: number one is feuding siblings; number two is members getting romantic. In a moment of weakness, I blurted out my feelings for my guitar player, Rig, and two years into our tenure, I fell into his bed.

Such a cliché, hoping to make harmony with a bandmate. I should have known better. It wasn't like MoonCraft was my first band. Our affair didn't last long before he'd moved on, leaving me to pretend everything was okay. Now Rig and our drummer, Halo, were *together* together and headed back to the U.S., most likely making plans for a new band without me.

Four years I'd invested in them. I'd told myself that if I could manage to keep us focused, this could be the project that launched my career into the stratosphere. Perhaps band killer rule three should be European club tour.

"What do you suggest I do?" It must have been the wine, or maybe he was responding to my downtrodden forlorn look, but as he gazed back at me intently, I thought, *It sure would be nice to not be alone tonight.*

He took my glass and set it down, then tugged gently on the lapel of my cardigan, frowning at a small hole in the seam where the shoulder met the sleeve. Yeah, I looked exactly as if I'd seen better days. "You could use a little comfort tonight, no? Save your worries for tomorrow?"

"You make it a habit of rescuing American musicians from trouble?"

"Most certainly not." His voice had a breathy tone, and it was higher-pitched than I would have thought by the way he got us out of a sticky situation. "I definitely don't make it a habit of kissing American musicians in trouble, but sometimes..."

"You make an exception?"

"Sí. Do you make a habit of needing rescue?"

"Not really? But I appreciate what you did tonight." I stepped closer to him, prompting him to put a hand on my waist, which, whatever, if this was going to happen he'd likely get a glimpse of what I *didn't* have going on. I might have winced though.

He gripped me a little tighter and his expression turned serious.

"You're safe here. That protest and the aftermath will likely go on for hours. You're welcome to stay, no expectations."

"But possibilities?"

He smiled then, and there was a mischievous glint in his soulful brown eyes.

"Endless."

I closed the distance between us, feeling the heat coming off of his hard chest under his tight t-shirt as our bodies came in contact. I relaxed for the first time in two weeks, and man, was it nice. People don't realize how much the lack of human contact and physical touch can really impact a person. Weigh them down or eliminate all ties they have until they blow away in the breeze.

He slid his hand around to my lower back and his fingers slipped under the waistband of my jeans.

"Then let's commence exploration."

His lips were the balm I needed, his tentative kisses soothing my soul from the losses I'd experienced, reminding me that there was still good in this world, still people willing to help out when you were in a rough patch, and right then, I was raw.

I also realized I wasn't thinking straight. Wasn't this how Americans went missing? I knew nothing about this guy, no one knew where I was. I still had a manager after this whole debacle, but she was back in the States and we weren't, like, besties or anything. I didn't talk to my family as they abhorred my career decisions. The only person back home who gave a damn about me was my former teacher, Mrs. Cecilia Galván. Perhaps it was time to reach out to her.

Well...tomorrow.

"Listen, Randall," he said, taking a strand of my long, curly hair, and winding it around his finger. "I can make up the sofa for you if you just want to rest—"

"And if I don't?" I ran my hands up his chest, balling the material of his t-shirt in my fists.

He tilted his head to the side and clicked his tongue against his teeth. "If you are sure, then I suggest we take this to bed."

His words unlocked a desire within me that hadn't seen the light of day for...a long time. He was direct, only slightly breathy in a way that let me know he was into this as much as I was, but he wasn't overtly flirtatious or attempting to seduce. He was a man on a mission, no time for superfluous chat. I liked it.

"Lead the way."

The next few minutes held a series of questions:

"Lights on or off?"

"Off," I said, wanting to experience this through my other four senses. Sight could be deceiving, and sometimes judgmental. And seeing when your partner was judging you was not a pleasant experience.

He must have had blackout curtains, though, because it was pitch black. Not even a digital clock. The only visible light came from his phone display, which he held in his hand.

"Music on or off?"

"On, please," I answered, wishing to hear what music he thought was perfect for sex. I didn't just make music for a living, but I experienced it holistically in all aspects of my life. Since he'd already mentioned Mike Patton, I wasn't surprised to hear another album he was featured on, *Lovage: Music to Make Love to Your Old Lady By*, playing through a speaker somewhere.

"Clothes?"

"Off."

"Mmm, excellent choice."

Once our clothes were removed and we fell into his bed, his hands were already exploring. Mine, too, and I'd been *so* right about the body beneath those clothes. The guy obviously made fitness a priority. I hoped he wasn't disappointed.

"Oral or no?"

"Oh, *yes*," I replied as he worked his way down my chest, his light stubble igniting my skin inch by inch until I was a quivering mess of want.

He held himself in a plank position, at least that's what it seemed like in the darkness, and the occasional grazing of skin against skin had me trembling. When he finally reached my straining erection, he didn't hesitate, just silently got to work. *Enthusiastically* got to work, making me shudder, and I praised him over and over. With everything that had gone wrong lately, having something go *so* right—

"Top or bottom?"

"Side, actually."

He moved back up my body and spoke close to my ear. "I'm afraid I'm not familiar—"

"Everything but...uh, *that*. Don't mind a little ass play, but no dick, yeah?"

"I hadn't heard that way of describing it before. I like it."

"I like *this*," I said, reaching for his cock, finally getting a moan from him. He was so quiet, I had to go by his pounding heart and his panting to know that he was feeling this too.

"I like this also." His accent was a little thicker, and his breathing sped up even more as I stroked him. He stopped moving for a moment, and I heard him fumble with a drawer next to the bed. I heard the click of a cap and then I felt cool liquid slide over my fingers. I chuckled.

"I like this better."

Then his slick hand was on my cock and we were moving together, mutual satisfaction on the menu. I was completely overwhelmed with stimuli; the music, his breath, the feel of his skin and the soft hair on his torso, the lube now warmed in our hands, the friction, his scent, something strong like Irish Spring soap that tickled my nose, the flavor of that fantastic wine on both of our tongues. So many sensations, and they were building into a crescendo that I wanted desperately to reach, and yet didn't want this feeling to end.

"This okay?" he asked.

"More than," I moaned, my body jerking under his. I pulled him down flush to me and he wrapped his other arm around me, turning us on our sides. I placed my free hand on his face, kissing him as best I could, though it was hard to focus. He took my thumb in his mouth and I groaned.

"Okay to come on you? I'm right there."

"Bé, we come together."

Our frantic movements lost their synchronicity and our pelvic bones bumped, his knuckles dug into my lower gut, and I loved it, that twinge of pain right before I—

"Molt be. Randall, fuck—"

"*Yessssss*," I hissed.

His face was pressed against mine, his lips moving halfway between kissing and speaking. He ran his fingers through our combined mess and then licked one. It was so hot that if it were at all physically possible, I would have come again. I grabbed for his face and kissed him hard, trying to express without words that this was more to me than just a hook-up. The combined tastes on his tongue of us, the wine...I'd remember these sensations for the rest of my life. Even if I never saw him again—a *him* I didn't even have a name for—he'd found me at a low point and he'd...cared. It meant a lot, this connection we'd made in his bed, under his sheets, skin against skin, even if it was just for one night.

"Can I get you anything?" he asked, his soft voice so kind. He sat up on the edge of the bed and I wished for the first time for just a little bit of light. I ran a hand down his back and paused when my fingers grazed...scar tissue? He flinched a bit and then stood up.

"Can you pause time?"

He chuckled, and I knew he'd moved away, but I heard nothing until the click of a soft lamp in the bathroom, which illuminated his gloriously naked body.

Oh. Heaven. Help me. Whatever I'd done to deserve to look upon his beauty, I was grateful for the opportunity.

He washed his hands, his lips drawn up in that quirk that alluded to humor but wasn't quite a smile. He turned to reach behind him for a towel and I saw what my fingers had grazed.

Were those *bullet wounds?* He also had a couple of long scars on his thigh that caught my eye as he turned to enter the bedroom.

Red flags? Maybe. But he'd done nothing to alarm me, and with how heavy my eyelids were, perhaps I was seeing things.

"Rest, amor. Tomorrow will present new opportunities."

I wanted to believe his words, but they were echoey, as if I was sliding down a tube away from him and into the darkness once more.

TWO

NOVEMBER 25, 2019
  7:42 AM Castelldefels, Catalonia, Spain

Two Weeks Later

What a difference a fortnight made.

I stood struggling to knot my stupid tie, the collar of my dress shirt already strangling me, in the tiny bathroom of my new apartment in Castelldefels, a town outside of Barcelona nearish to the airport. I had purchased exactly six dress shirts, six ties, and six pairs of chinos to start my new job teaching music at the Frederick Douglass International School.

And it was all thanks to my savior. Well, the *can-do* attitude was thanks to him. The job was thanks to my old teacher, Cecilia Galván.

"Randall! What happened? Tell me everything!"

I'd called her after my appointment at the embassy, which went relatively smoothly, and told her everything...the band squabbles, the theft, the decision to break up—okay, not every-thing. I didn't tell her about my tryst. Not that I hadn't shared my boy troubles with her in the past, and I'd been there for her when she first split up with her ex-husband two years prior, so we understood each other. But that experience wasn't one I was ready to share with anyone yet.

The clerk at the embassy said that as long as I was employed, I could stay, and honestly I wasn't done with Spain. My mystery man had made me think twice about leaving on a bad note. I loved it here, and if I was going to start a new life, why not do it in this exciting place?

"So I've got a little time to find a job, and I was wondering, I know you spent some time here with Mr. Segura—"

"You know what I'm going to say," she'd started. I did know.

"That I should finally put my teaching credential to use." I'd earned my music degree at UC Berkeley, which she'd encouraged me to pursue, and managed to do my student teaching while getting the first of my three bands together. I knew at that time I wasn't *ready* ready to be in the classroom. I wanted to give a music career a shot. She'd understood, though she told me she hoped I would find my way back to teaching eventually. Claimed I was a natural. *Okay, Mrs. Galvan.*

"Yes, and there are so many ways you could do that in Spain. There are programs to teach English, international schools, au pair... Wait, I've got a number here...I met this woman at the vineyard, they were having an event, a fundraiser, and Felip's cousin Fermín introduced us. She's the principal of an American international school in Castelldefels. I could reach out..."

"That would be great." I'd try anything at this point. I wasn't normally the kind of person to wallow, and I'd done it for two weeks at that point.

"Great! Let me give her a call, and you know, there's always the winery? It's physical labor, but you've never shied from that."

"No, ma'am. I'm seriously willing to do anything at this point. I just want to work and put all this shit behind me."

"Ma'am," she snorted. "Awesome. Let me call her and I'll let you know what she says! In the meantime, get that resume going and I'll dust off the letter of recommendation I wrote for you before you became a rock star." She laughed, and it cheered me even more. It was nice knowing that someone had faith in me when my band hadn't. When the label hadn't. When my family hadn't. Good ole Mrs. Galván, soon-to-be Segura. She'd found her second chance at happiness in Spain. Maybe so could I.

She called me back the next day and said her contact was thrilled to meet with me, and the arrangements were made in a blur. I took the bus out to Castelldefels, aced the interview, had a tour of the music department, which had been without a teacher since the beginning of the year, much to the chagrin of the parents, and I was offered the job on the spot. Seeing as it was November, they needed time to rearrange student sched-ules and to give them time to sign up.

Felip's cousin Fermín had an empty apartment in one of his complexes between the beach and the school, and I moved in with my scarce belongings that had survived the theft.

I was going to be teaching all grade levels, both vocal and instrumental music. I had a week between getting hired and getting myself reacquainted with the wind and brass instru-ments, as well as how the heck to teach little ones what had been ingrained in my brain from an early age. Piano at five, guitar at ten, voice at twelve, clarinet and sax from twelve to eighteen...eventually settling on guitar and keyboards for my pursuit of rock stardom. I'd been lucky I had such a varied back-ground. It meant teaching should come easy.

Right.

Kids.

No problem.

I'd channel Mrs. Galván and hope for the best.

Throughout this time of pep talks from her, settling the band's affairs with our manager, Cherish, having my apartment in LA packed up and put into storage from afar, which Cherish oversaw, thank goodness...I'd thought about *him* every spare moment.

I'd woken up at some point early that next morning and he'd been gone. Unsure how to handle all the awkward morning-after stuff since I hadn't really done this before, especially not in a foreign country, I'd left him a note, my number, and thanked him with a goofy, spontaneous poem:

You found me in the darkness
And gave me shelter
You met me in the darkness
And brought me peace
You left me in the darkness
But this night gave me hope
And when I leave your darkness
With a smile upon my face
I will not fear the darkness
Only wonder of his name

It was a bit much, but I hadn't been inspired to write much in the past year. Now, I was inspired to do all sorts of things.

I'd doubted that he would call, but hoped that perhaps, in this city of however many million people, our paths might cross again. Who knew? Once I got my bearings, maybe I'd do some solo club gigs. Maybe he'd show up. Maybe we'd bond over music.

Maybe I needed to focus on the task at hand.

Randall Sutter 2.0

Who needed YouTube to help him figure out how to tie a tie.

I grabbed a cronut from the box I'd picked up at my local panaderia and shoved it in my face as I walked out to ride my new bike to school. I raised the kickstand and swung my messenger bag over my back as I pushed off from the curb. I felt like a kid on his first day, minus my old SpongeBob lunch box that had been my older brother's. Hand-me-downs had been the norm in the Sutter family.

My new boss, Principal Lara Trujillo-Perez, reminded me a lot of Mrs. Galván—it was still weird to call her Cecilia. Lara also exuded that welcoming energy and made me feel like I *wasn't* about to take a huge leap that I wasn't qualified to take. Despite me nearly trying to talk her out of offering me a job, she had been downright giddy over having a well-known young music teacher who had performance cred and had even had a Billboard-charting/Grammy-award-winning album. MoonCraft might be over, but my foray into the music business, she said, made me uniquely qualified for the position.

"Many of the students we get are seeing artists on social media take off with their creative endeavors. You're someone who represents the reality of hard work and dedication that can get you far in this world."

Uh, yeah, it can also get you stranded in Spain with no money, no boyfriend, and ready to take a job you said you'd never do. I guess that could be considered a win? Whatever. I was determined to make this new job work and to do right by the kids, as my music teachers had done by me.

It wasn't that I didn't want to work with kids. I loved kids. I'd just never wanted to fail. I was trying hard to look at this as a detour and not a derailment.

I pulled into the parking lot of the school, which seemed to be a repurposed factory of some kind. There was a series of white buildings with decorative brick inlay and lots of glass and greenery. The interior was quite modern and set up in a way to encourage collaboration between students, almost like a coffee shop vibe or a workroom on an Apple campus. Lots of tech, lots of vibrant colors and greenery, and lots of inspirational quotes painted on the walls in all different languages.

Mrs. Lara Trujillo-Perez said she would meet me this morning to go over my classes and then the kids would arrive at 8:30. I could do this. I could—

I'd been so preoccupied with my can-do thoughts that I missed a low curb. My tire hit, stopping the bike, but my body continued its momentum and I flew into the bushes. My messenger bag, carrying my new laptop I'd purchased with the money I'd gotten from the band settlement, smacked me in the head and the bushes tore at my new clothes along with my favorite cardigan.

"Nice, Sutter."

I heard the rapid clicking of heels and rolling wheels of some sort.

"Oh my goodness! Randall! Are you all right?"

Awesome for my new boss to find me in the bushes.

I managed to get myself to standing and brush the leaves and twigs off my clothes before turning around to smile confidently—

Mrs. Trujillo-Perez was hurrying forward with the custodian...who had a very familiar chin dimple.

"Oh, your poor bike! Don't worry, we've got a bike shop near here. I'll send it with one of the aides to see if they can repair it, but you... Oh, you poor thing!"

The custodian wore coveralls and a ball cap pulled down low over his eyes, but there was no mistaking that chin dimple, which in the light of day I could tell was not only what was probably a hereditary beauty mark, but he also had a scar there. I had so many questions.

I almost didn't care that I'd hurled myself into the bushes on my first day. Not if it meant seeing him again.

He handed me a tissue and pointed toward my cheek.

Mrs. Trujillo-Perez spoke to him in Spanish while I tried to pick the rest of the bushes out of my hair, which I'd pulled back in a bun for the day and would now need to be brushed and redone.

"Alonso will take your bike for you. Here, let me get your bag. Are you sure you're all right? Are you hurt?"

"Surprisingly, no," I said, and I meant it. Other than the stinging on my cheek.

The custodian—Alonso? I *liked* that—said something to Mrs. Trujillo-Perez in rapid Spanish, and I only caught the words for cheek, mejilla, and blood, sangre. I wiped at my cheek and yes, I had a nasty scratch.

"Oh, it's okay. Scars build character, right?" I tried to laugh it off. Nothing was going to ruin this day, not even a trashed bike and a humiliating fall. Nope. I had a job, I had a new purpose... and I'd found *him*.

Alonso.

Muy bien, gracias.

He took my bike by the handlebars and tried to push it but the frame was bent, so he hefted the thing up over his shoulder as if it were a five-pound sack of potatoes and carried it off toward what must have been the delivery bay, as it had large rolling doors.

"I'm so sorry. Are you sure you're okay?"

"I'm great, Mrs. Trujillo-Perez—"

"Oh, call me Lara when it's us," she said, wrinkling her nose. She was probably in her late thirties/early forties, like Mrs. Galván. Tall, long black hair, accent seemed to be California, maybe? She certainly spoke beautiful Spanish. I, on the other hand, could understand bits and pieces, but when I spoke it, I sounded like the worst gringo.

"Alonso said he will take care of your bike himself. Don't worry. He's quite capable."

That he is. Perhaps he hadn't recognized me in the daylight, but no matter. He was here. At my new job.

I couldn't stop smiling.

The kids were awesome. I don't know what I expected, other than a bunch of uniformed hooligans, but with the exception of some running in the hallways and a spilled water bottle on the carpet in my classroom, it really had been okay. I recalled a lot of the classroom management tricks I'd learned while student teaching, plus I had the benefit of teaching a subject that for many kids was a break from learning subjects they struggled with. There was the occasional kid who shared they were there because their parents made them take music, but most of the kids, especially the older ones, perked up when I mentioned teaching them things about the business, about recording and mixing using tools on their computers, and that we would not only be doing classic pieces but more contemporary scores, like those written by Danny Elfman and Trent Reznor.

All of the kids spoke English, I'd been assured, but many had other first languages including Spanish, Catalan, French, Arabic, Hausa from Nigeria, Italian, and a few spoke Ukrainian. I had so many plans for how to get the kids invested, including studying folk and pop music from their countries of origin, and even composing music of their own before the year was out.

I had two sections of choir with the littles in the morning, followed by two sections of instrumental with the older kids, and after lunch I had middle-grade choir and instrumental.

That was my schedule three days a week, then two days a week I would teach private lessons to students whose parents requested. Lara wanted me to consider adding afterschool chorus for the older students, when I was settled of course, and for an additional stipend, and I had plans for implementing a performance program where the kids could practice playing their instruments live with other musicians and cut their teeth on what it means to be a professional musician.

Lara had explained to me that at the end of the day, the parents would come to the classroom to pick up their children from me. There was a dedicated terminal next to the door and I needed to stand there and make sure every kid was signed out before they left. As some of our students were high-profile, the school took extra precautions with their safety. Some parents even hired private security for their children, so Lara told me not to be alarmed if I saw adults in the hallway. They wore special ID badges, but it was a bit jarring to see them carrying weapons in a school. These weren't rent-a-cop security like back in the States. Who the heck were these families?

My imagination ran wild, wondering what kind of kids we were talking about. Children of diplomats? Celebrities? Military? Billionaires? I doubted that, but who knew? I had been just as excited to meet the parents as I was the kids.

I was in my spot at the podium near the door when school ended on that first day and the kids lined up, coming forward when their parent or designee arrived. The special computer system had a scanner that would match the person to the kid. No match, no kid was leaving. One of the moms, I think, recognized me, as her eyes widened and she twirled her hair around her finger as she gestured for her kid to come forward. She fumbled with her ID, dropping it on the ground and apologizing. I hadn't expected there to be anyone more nervous than me there that day.

Pickup went pretty smoothly, and I had to admit to myself that I'd been looking around corners all day for Alonso, and now that school was out, I intended to go looking for him...

Until my nerves got the best of me.

What if he honestly didn't remember me?

What if he *had* recognized me and blew me off? Like, he really planned for us to only be for a night and seeing me again was a complication he didn't want?

What if...

I peeked out into the hallway and there was my bike. Fixed. It had to have been difficult to repair it and yet, there it was. Guess I wouldn't be walking home.

I wanted to thank him, but then I heard my name called.

"Oh, Monsieur Sutter? Monsieur Sutter, I'm Madame Lahlou, I am in charge of personnel." She held out her hand to me and gave a little nod. "We have some paperwork for you, monsieur. Please come with me." She was an older African woman wearing a plum-colored long-sleeved dress and matching headscarf. She turned and walked at a fast clip and I had to jog to catch up with her.

"How was your first day?"

"Great! Really, the kids are fun."

She nodded but continued to face forward. "I have found that it is not the children who are a problem in this school but the adults." She raised an eyebrow and glanced my way. "Many of the parents send their assistants and au pairs to collect the students and they tend to make a fuss over having to show identification."

"Do we really need to worry so much about security?"

We'd reached the office and she paused at the door.

"While I admit our students do not have to worry about such things as American children do, there are still dangers when the identity of your family is exposed, attending a school primarily for expats but with a contingent of local celebrities and wealthy families. We have carefully screened all of our students and their families, but one never knows. Other international schools have had children targeted for politically motivated kidnappings. We work very hard to ensure that does not happen here."

"That sounds terrifying," I said quietly. Now I understood the need for the bodyguards and the check-out system.

A clatter startled me, and I turned around to see Alonso picking up a mop from the floor and darting into a classroom. Hopefully this paper-signing business would be quick and I could track him down after.

Or should I play it cool?

Should I wait—

"Right this way, monsieur."

"Right, sorry."

Madame Lahlou smiled and held the door open for me. She had such a beautiful voice, I found myself wanting to keep speaking to her, even though she seemed busy. I could get lost listening to people with certain tones or musicality to their speech, just as I did when I listened to music.

She laid the papers out on her desk and I signed, admittedly, without paying enough attention to them.

"We received your California teaching credentials, but as Madame Trujillo-Perez informed you, you will be considered a probationary employee until you have applied for and received your permit to teach in a private setting. That is this form here," she said, pointing it out as if she'd caught me signing without reading. I should be better about signing contracts, I knew that. Thankfully I hadn't been screwed by our band contracts. Cherish took good care of me in that regard.

"Thank you, I appreciate all of the help."

She nodded. "It is my duty to assist you. Here is your staff handbook, as I am not sure you received one. We normally go over it at our orientation for new staff, but as you are starting later in the year, you should go over it yourself. I would also like to invite you to our social gathering on Friday after school. We go to a restaurant near the beach or in town for tapas and drinks. Usually an email goes around with the location for the week. It will be a good time for you to meet the rest of the staff."

And perhaps a good time to see—no, I needed to focus on work and doing a good job with these kids. If Alonso came around, maybe.

"One more thing, monsieur?"

"Yes?"

She glanced around the office, which was mostly empty except for the secretary who was on the phone at her desk, and I heard voices coming from Lara's office.

Madame Lahlou stepped closer and lowered her voice.

"While I encourage you to associate with your colleagues, beware of fraternizing with them, as well as with parents or their help. It is our protocol. Madame Trujillo-Perez is quite supportive of her staff, but crossing the line of appropriate behavior with a member of our school community could be a cause for concern for someone who is on probation."

I nodded. Good to know what I was dealing with.

"Thanks for the advice."

It was probably for the best, then, that neither Alonso nor his cart were anywhere to be seen when I left the office a few minutes later. I rode my bike home, taking much more care with my surroundings, and once there I scarfed down a leftover meal from a local Italian restaurant, and got to work going over the first-day surveys. Hopefully I'd be able to stay awake long enough.

THREE

FRIDAY 3:58 PM Frederick Douglass International School, Castelldefels, Catalonia, Spain

My classes were great, but private lessons allowed me to really get to know the kids on an individual level and gauge each of the students' interest in music. A few of them shared interesting perspectives.

"I want to be a pop star and make enough money to pay for any plastic surgery I might need as I get older."

"I want to be in a band that has mosh pits. I like the violence."

"I'm going to be a rapper. My mom says I'm great at it."

And my favorite:

"I'm going to be a lead singer so I can have a beautiful date every night."

Good luck, kid.

On the other hand, there were a few who had admirable goals.

"I want to write music for people who are hurting."

"I want to use my songs to bring about real change and challenge people's problematic beliefs."

But my most memorable conversation happened in my very last private lesson with a boy named Pere Ferrer.

"I want to be able to play with my father. He is a world-famous flamenco guitarist. He met Paco de Lucia before. He plays all over the world."

"That's pretty great, Pere. So you want to learn more on guitar? You're already pretty good." He was. He'd shown me what he could do and he already had great form and knew a lot of the techniques that made flamenco players stand out. And who was I to teach a virtuoso's kid?

"Maybe, but maybe I could learn piano or accordion so I can accompany him. Then maybe he'll let me tour with him and we can be together always."

"I'm happy to teach you whatever you want to learn." With each student on this first day, we made up quarterly goals that were attainable, measurable, and specific. I wanted these kids to have success.

Pere wanted to learn one of his father's songs on piano to surprise him.

"Let's make that our stretch goal, okay?" If he hadn't had any training, playing a whole song in two and a half months was a lot to ask.

We spent the rest of our time getting familiar with the piano and how to translate the music from guitar to keys. I was having a blast with the funny little ten-year-old and I didn't hear we had company.

"Pere, are you keeping your teacher after hours? Ay, this boy. He will talk your ear off if you let him."

"Papa," Pere said and he ran for the man in the doorway, who had yet to check in.

"Get your stuff, son. We've got to pick up your stepmother and get to the airport."

Pere's whole mood soured. "I thought she was not coming?"

Mr. Ferrer patted his head and gave his hunched-over shoulder a push toward the lockers.

Pere scowled as he went to get his things from his locker, moving at a glacial pace.

"I understand senyora Trujillo-Perez landed us a real rock star to teach our kids." The guy strummed an air guitar and curled his lip a la Billy Idol then laughed. "I'm teasing you. I'm Paolo Ferrer. It's nice to have you here."

I shook his hand and didn't let him ruffle me. I had actually heard of him before, but I refused to be starstruck. He was close to six feet tall, thin with deeply tanned skin and expensively shabby clothes draped fashionably, including a cashmere scarf knotted around his neck and Italian loafers. His wavy light brown hair was thinning around the hairline and his bedroom hazel eyes probably garnered him favor with his chosen lovers.

He oozed arrogance. And he was giving off condescension that left a bad taste in my mouth.

"It's great to be here."

"You were in a popular indie rock band, weren't you? In America?"

"We did all right."

A streak of navy blue moved behind Mr. Ferrer and then Alonso was in my classroom. While I was trying not to freak out in front of an apparently world-famous parent.

"We'll have to play together sometime," he said, and my neck broke out into a sweat beneath my stuffy collar.

"That would be amazing, thank you. Well, I don't want to keep you, you have a plane to catch." *And I'm trying to catch the custodian before he disappears again.*

All I'd seen of Alonso was flashes the past two days. I hadn't even been able to thank him for fixing my bike.

"Of course, no it's a shame we are leaving this weekend, but soon, perhaps."

And I was stuck between a real international rock star and the man who'd rocked my world, totally unsure how to proceed. If the no-fraternizing rule was a *thing* thing, and I admitted that I would jam with this guy, would Alonso rat me out? How did I bow out of this?

"I appreciate the invitation."

Ferrer looked me up and down as his son trudged his way. He tried to be all affectionate with Pere, but the kid wasn't having it.

"Oh, Mr. Ferrer? Your ID please." Thank goodness I snapped out of it. I'd hate to fuck up on my first week and let a kid go without an ID.

And then his façade slipped and I got a look at the real Ferrer.

"Right, right." He patted his pockets and frowned. "I'm afraid I don't have my wallet. Must have left it with the driver. Come on, Pere."

"But, sir? If you'll hold on a moment." I panicked. "Ah, Alonso? Can you please call for Mrs. Trujillo-Perez on your radio?"

Alonso's eyes shot to me and then to Ferrer and he shrugged. "No inglés."

What the fuck?

He carried the trash can hurriedly toward his cart outside the door. Ferrer said something to him in gruff-sounding Spanish. Or was it Catalan? I was still trying to figure out the difference. Alonso kept his eyes lowered and nodded as he left the room.

"He'll bring her, but honestly, I can't really wait around. Do you have a phone in this classroom?"

Poor Pere was beet red in the cheeks below his mop of dark curls. He looked as if he wished he could be anywhere else.

"Sure, sure. My apologies," I said. "I'm new and I don't want to break with procedure. You understand, right?"

I moved over to the desk and picked up the phone to dial the front office.

"Oui monsieur?"

"Oh, um, this is—"

"Can I help you?"

"Ah, senyor Ferrer," Lara said as she came inside the room, saving me from the wrath of an angry, entitled parent. I apologized to Mrs. Lahlou and hung up the phone.

"Bona tarda, senyora." He kissed her cheek and she stood stiffly as if she hated to be rude but she really hated him touching her.

"Senyor Sutter has been instructed to phone us if anyone is without ID. You understand the need for our protocols, verdad?"

"Sí," he said, following her out the door looking annoyed.

"Goodbye Pere," I called out as they left. The boy turned and gave me a sad wave before following his father to the office.

In the melee, Alonso had disappeared again. I trotted out to the hallway, only to see him turning the corner at the far end. If I called out it would echo and disturb anyone else still in the building.

Well, damn. If he was going to keep avoiding me, I would just find a way to leave him a gift as a thank you for the bike. It was the least I could do.

But what was that about him not speaking English? Bullshit. He spoke just fine when he was...when we were...

Oh for fuck's sake. If he wanted to pretend like he didn't

know me, whatever. Maybe he too was trying to follow the no-fraternizing protocol. Maybe he thought, foolishly, that I'd look down on him for his job? That was ridiculous, and also pretty fucking entitled for me to even think that.

A moment later, the Ferrers left the office, Pere with his head down while his father scolded him, and they walked out the front doors of the building.

"Randall!" Lara trotted toward me, her heels clackety-clacking down the hall. "Excellent work. You did the right thing." When she got closer, she took a deep breath. "Most of our parents are wonderful, but then there are those..."

"I understand. I got distracted though and I almost forgot to check. He's..."

"A bit much, yeah. He's a very big deal and the type to get people in the community stirred up, if you know what I mean."

I figured I should be upfront. "He asked to play together. I understand there are rules..."

"Ah. Well, I'd understand if you wanted to—" She laughed when she saw me shake my head vigorously. "Or, you could tell him it's protocol, that we don't see families for social events outside of school."

"I like that. Thank you. I'll do that if it comes up again."

She smiled knowingly at me then her eyes flared. "You are coming to our social this evening? Are you ready? You can ride with me and Max, our physical education teacher."

I glanced around. Other than seeing Alonso, I had nothing else to do. "Let me grab my bag."

The staff at Frederick Douglass was just as diverse as the students. There were six of us Americans, three young teachers from France, who apparently shared an apartment in the same complex where I lived, and several Catalan-speaking teachers, who corrected me when I assumed that only folks living in Catalonia spoke Catalan. Turned out there was a whole-ass country called Andorra across the border, and most of the country spoke Catalan, not to mention there were Catalan speakers in France and in other parts of Spain outside of Catalonia. They even tried to teach me the differences between Catalan and Castellano—things like greetings and where to put accents, which of course was different between the two languages even on similar words—that even with my weak Spanish, I should be able to pick up. And boy did they like to spill the tea.

"Yeah, that Ferrer is a piece of work," Ivan said, a tall, slim guy from Brooklyn who I discovered shared a love of music. Ivan played drums for a jazz quartet back home. "He pulled that 'hey let's jam' card with me, too, and when I said no, he said it was probably for the best. Didn't want the kids to see their teacher shown up."

"Wow," I said. "And his son is so sweet."

"Oh, oui, he really is." Josette, who taught English and French, clicked her tongue against her teeth. "So sad. His mother is so very kind. They were divorced two years ago and she was here for the rest of that school year, but then she had to go back to Morocco. Pere was very close to her. I helped him write letters to her in French."

My heart hurt for the little kid. I hated to think that he would work so hard to try to impress his father when the guy obviously wouldn't see his efforts.

"Senyor Ferrer is a menace," one of the local teachers said, and a whole conversation erupted in Catalan, to which Lara held up a hand.

"Take care with your words. There may be big ears. If any of you have further issues with him, please send him to me."

The Catalan speakers glanced around and apologized in

hushed voices.

"No need," she said with a kind smile. "All good. Now, Randall, since you're joining us mid-year, tell us more about you since we're all bored with each other."

Everyone laughed, but one of the French women touched my arm and said, "What I really want to know is what happened to your band? I remember seeing you guys on the MTV Europe Awards!"

To add to my mortification, the three French women all started singing our last top twenty hit, "Trouble Kind."

"Now, everyone, be nice to Randall," Lara said, placing her hand on my back as she set a shot glass in front of me. "Let him settle in before you start attacking him, chismosas."

I barked out a laugh at her use of the word for gossips.

"We want him to stick around," Lara stage whispered. The staff all held up their drinks and she addressed the group. "A toast to Randall Sutter. Thank you for bringing music back to our school."

Everyone cheered, I downed that shot, which turned out to be tequila, and two more. I was feeling really happy about Randall Sutter 2.0 when suddenly my music was playing over the sound system to the bar, Josette was dragging me out to dance, and then we took the party out to the beach, where I dipped my toes in the Mediterranean for the very first time.

A nearly full moon hung low in the sky and I took in a deep breath.

This was good. I liked this. I'd made a good decision to stay here. Too bad the one who'd inspired my reinvention wasn't beside me.

But then, perhaps his only role had been to get me out of danger and into this 2.0 phase. I'd be grateful for what I had in my life. A new job, new friends, and a new home in a lively and exciting place. It was up to me to make it great.

FOUR

SUNDAY 7:43 AM CASTELLDEFELS, Catalonia, Spain

Half of my first weekend as a teacher in Spain was spent hungover. My new colleagues thought it was hilarious that I got so inebriated on just a few shots and vowed to break me into the world of drinking like an authentic European. I went with my new French friends Josette, Camille, and Sasha to brunch on Sunday, and it was so nice to have the company. I didn't even mind that they fussed over me. It made me realize that my band had been on the outs for a lot longer than I'd thought. When was the last time we'd gone out to eat together? Or explored the areas around our gigs? Once we got to our destinations, Rig and Halo would go off by themselves exploring and rarely invited me to join them for meals. I'd hang out with our tech, Bruno, and our driver, Medium Mike, or wander by myself.

Randall Sutter 2.0 suddenly had friends, and it was nice.

As we were walking back to our complex, we passed a liquor store and I had an idea.

"Oh, hey, I need to grab a bottle of wine."

They followed me in, curious.

"What's the occasion?" Sasha asked.

"I wanted to thank Alonso for fixing my bike."

"Oh! That's right. You are quite lucky you were not hurt. I heard it was a terrible fall," Josette said, patting my arm.

"Thank you. Would have been tough to teach music with a broken arm. Hey, do any of you know him?" I stopped in front of the wine display and saw a familiar bottle. A cabernet from Segura International. I was pretty sure it was the stuff Alonso'd had that night. I grabbed two bottles, one for him and one for myself.

The three women giggled. "No, I'm afraid," Josette said. "Camille tried to invite him to come to Friday Social but he declined."

Camille sighed. "So sad. He's quite beautiful behind those caps he wears."

"Has he been at the school long?" I tried to sound vaguely interested. I shouldn't have been digging, but these three seemed to be a font of information about everyone. They'd already told me who was dating who despite the fraternization rules, and they let me know that more than one mother had already asked about my relationship status.

"Alas, I am a lone gay wolf. Not cougar bait."

They burst out laughing and all hugged me.

"Well then, we shall have to keep our eyes open," Josette said, waggling her eyebrows. "Alonso came a few weeks or so ago? Never speaks to anyone, only to Lara, so I cannot confirm his status."

"Oh, no, that's okay," I said, trying to play like I wasn't hanging on her every word. I happened to know that Alonso was into men, but I wasn't about to admit that to them, nor how I knew. My little secret.

"I'll admit this to only you three," Camille said. "He's shit at cleaning. He can fix things well enough, but I vacuum my own carpet and clean my own desks now."

"Does it really matter how well he cleans, though?" Sasha said demurely. "He contributes so much beauty to our school, don't you think?"

"Definitely." Josette said. "A one-man beautification committee."

The three women giggled again, completely aware they were being ridiculous. They weren't mean-spirited at all in their appreciation for Alonso. I was pleased they'd taken me under their wing. It had been a long time since I'd had a group of women friends.

The subject changed as I paid for my purchases to whether any of them were going to go home for the holidays. We were back to our complex before it was my turn to answer that, no, I would not be going back to the States anytime soon. I thanked them for inviting me to brunch, and after all the hugs and cheek kisses I was still getting used to, I went up to my apartment, cracked open the bottle I'd bought for myself and sighed as I realized it was exactly the right one.

Inspired, I pulled out a brand-new notebook and put pen to paper. Without a band in mind, I was free to write whatever kind of music I was feeling. The words that began to come out of me were hopeful, curious, flirty. How to know the *all* of another person. If Alonso wasn't going to acknowledge me, I could wonder. The possibilities were indeed endless.

The next morning I arrived early and snuck into the custodian's workroom. I located a desk where there were a few left-over condiment packs and napkins, which I assumed was where he ate. I was about to set the bottle, in a brown paper bag, and the mostly blank thank you card that I'd merely signed my name to on the desk, when I noticed a student schedule printout sticking out from the top drawer. Pere Ferrer's schedule.

Why would Alonso have Pere's schedule?

I opened the drawer and there was also a printout of his demographic screen, with his address and list of emergency contacts. What would the custodian be doing with student information like that?

Sure, I was the one snooping, but that didn't make my discovery any less suspect.

I checked my watch and realized my first student appointment would be arriving in fifteen minutes and I hadn't yet organized all of my sheet music for the day. I turned on my heel and sped out of the custodian's room—

And smacked right into Alonso.

His eyes went wide. I couldn't help the flutters in my stomach—equal parts excited and suspicious, but then...what was I supposed to say?

"I'm sorry, excuse me," I said.

"¿Necesitas ayuda?"

That voice. I fucking melted into a puddle of sensory memory. It washed over me like—

"Señor Sutter? Necesitas ayuda?" he asked with an irritated tone, not making eye contact.

"Um, no, gracias."

The flutters in my gut crashed to the bottom and sat so heavily I might as well have had a brick in there. Why was he being like this?

He opened his mouth to say something else when a group of kids came running into the hall, distracting us both. I turned to tell the kids not to run, and when I turned back, he'd gone around me and slipped into the custodian's room. I wanted to see the look on his face when he saw my gift. That would tell me whether or not he'd been hit over the head or something and didn't remember me. But he shut the door.

How could he act like we were strangers? We'd been so

good together, or was that just my imagination? Was I such a bad lay? So easily forgettable? Maybe I should add this to the list of causes for bands to break up: Rule Four, forgettable front man. God, could my ego take any more of this shit?

I trudged back to my classroom in a foul mood, only to find Pere Ferrer sitting outside on the ground, looking more miserable than me.

"Pere? What's the matter?"

He perked up. "Bon dia, senyor Sutter. I was hoping I could stay with you this morning? I don't have class until after morning break and I usually go to the library, but I was hoping I could practice on the piano with my headphones?"

Aw, my first little teacher's pet. "That would be fine with me, Pere, but you should get a note from the librarian. I don't want either of us to get in trouble."

His face lit up and he nodded. "I'll go see Mademoiselle Arnault for a note." He ran for the door and I called out for him not to run, but he was out the door before I finished speaking.

A little girl with colorful hair ties in her braided hair peeked in, her round dark eyes obviously spooked by the boy running out of my room like a bat out of hell. "Boys, am I right? Always causing a ruckus!"

That made her smile. She carried her messenger bag in front of her as if to protect herself.

"Wait! Don't tell me." She froze in place, her smile gone. "You must be Lissette Lokoto?"

She nodded and took two steps closer.

I bowed to her and she laughed.

"Welcome to music lessons. What would you like to learn today?"

"I want to learn to sing like Beyonce." She linked her fingers behind her back and swayed back and forth.

"All right. Beyonce is sure fantastic, but how about you

learn to sing like Lissette Lokoto?"

She frowned. "What do you mean?"

"I mean, how about you learn to sing the best that Lissette Lokoto can sing, and if you want to sing Beyonce's songs, well, that's your choice. But I think all singers need to discover the voice of their soul, don't you? And you find that by learning to sing all kinds of songs."

She blinked a couple of times and then she nodded. "Uh-huh. I would like that, too."

So we got down to it, and the moment she opened her mouth to sing, I knew Beyonce herself would have bowed to this little queen. She had an incredible instrument at a mere eleven years old. I got the tingles all over just thinking of what she and I could accomplish together.

Thanks a lot, Cecilia Galvan. You were right. I am a natural teacher.

The second week of teaching was exhilarating and exhausting at the same time. I wondered when the honeymoon period would end? These kids were different than the kids I'd taught during my student teaching, but all kids had the potential to get goofy, I knew that. Cecilia used to say, "Never Smile before Thanksgiving," but since I'd started my job later in the year—and that holiday wasn't even celebrated in this country—did I wait until after the winter holidays?

I spent some of my lunch periods eating in the cafeteria with the other teachers, but Thursday and Friday, I needed a break from peopling so I went outside for a walk. I may have been the front man of a band, but my introverted self could only handle so much. The weather was decent, and with my old trusty cardigan it was warm enough. The school was a few blocks from the beach, a little far for me to walk on my lunch break, but I found a pedestrian bridge close by that I could stand on and see the Mediterranean Sea.

It was wild to think that I was living on the far side of the world from where I had grown up. Yes, I'd been all over the States and Europe with MoonCraft, but this was a whole new experience. I wasn't just seeing the sights. I was embedded in a new community. I had new friends for the first time in a long time. Randall Sutter 2.0 was…pleasantly content.

I breathed in the fresh air and was about to return to the school when I looked down from the pedestrian bridge and saw two big black SUVs with tinted windows turning into the school parking lot. They stopped in the middle of the driveway and the drivers of both cars got out and opened the passenger doors, almost synchronized.

Out of the first car came a stocky, middle-aged man in a blazer with his thin hair buzzed to the scalp, and in the second car was Mr. Ferrer and a young woman, perhaps the stepmother Pere mentioned? Ferrer and the woman walked over to the older man, they greeted with kisses on the cheek, and then the two men launched into a heated conversation with lots of gesturing and frowning. The woman appeared bored, scrolling on her phone, only occasionally looking up.

I caught the sight of movement on the sidewalk in front of the school—and there was Alonso, slowly pushing his cart while casually glancing the way of the conversation. The men looked his way only briefly and then continued to talk.

A car pulled up and the driver honked when he couldn't get past the SUVs. He climbed out of his sedan and stormed toward Ferrer and the other man. The SUV drivers—who looked like the quintessential action movie bodyguards—moved to block his way, but then they allowed him into their conversation. There was finger pointing, and then he stormed away from Ferrer and the stocky man.

Alonso had continued walking and was now pushing his cart toward the driveway.What the heck? Why were they here in the middle of the day and arguing in the school parking lot? It wasn't even pickup time.

Then I saw Lara come out of the doors and walk toward them as if on a mission, her flowing black skirt whipping around her high-heeled boots, her long black hair flicking behind her. That was my cue to stop spying and make my way back to campus to be sure Lara was...safe? What did I think I was going to do, bust into the scene like some sort of Jason Statham action star and save the day?

It didn't matter. She might need backup, and while I fully believed that women were perfectly capable of standing up for themselves, everyone could use an ally. I took off at a jog, determined to be there in case she needed help. I took the steps down off of the pedestrian bridge two at a time, kept up a good pace down the street toward the school, and then slowed to a brisk walk as I turned the corner onto the driveway. I was hidden from view, as there were tall shrubs next to the school at the entrance...so Alonso didn't see me approaching. He had a phone to his ear and was speaking in a low voice.

"Sí. Ambròs Vidal. Sí. I have pictures. No, the boy is inside the school. I cannot get close enough to tell, but the parent who approached them was unhappy, said the school parking lot was no place for separatist propaganda. Sí. Ah, merda. The principal is out now. I will go to her. I'll meet you after. Sí. Adéu."

No inglés my ass.

Something very strange was going on with Alonso. Who had he been talking—no, *reporting* to? And in English? This, plus the schedule I'd found in his office. The hair on the back of my neck stood up and I thought about what Madame Lahlou had said, about high-profile kids and the dangers of kidnapping. Was that what was going on here?

Was Alonso watching the Ferrers because he wanted Pere?

I didn't have time to work out any more scenarios in my mind. I came around the bushes as Alonso approached Lara and spoke to her in Catalan. I think. I couldn't make out enough words to tell what he was saying. She frowned and nodded to him, then turned to the parents.

"I welcome all members of our Frederick Douglass community to visit the school at appropriate times, but I'd appreciate it if you would hold your conversations off school grounds. Some of the parents have voiced concerns."

Ferrer bowed dramatically to her. "No need to worry, senyora Trujillo-Perez," he said, exaggerating the Spanish pronunciation of her name. "Senyor Vidal and I were just about to grab a café together. The school was a logical place to meet in the middle. Geographically it is central to us both."

"Thank you. We'll see you at pickup," she said, nodding to both men before she turned on her heel and followed Alonso into the school, the two of them carrying on a conversation in low voices. Lara caught my eye as she walked in but continued speaking to Alonso after the doors closed behind them.

The black SUVs passed me by and Ferrer saluted me from the passenger window.

What in the fuck was happening?

The only clue I received was a staff email at the end of the workday:

Dear Staff:

In light of a situation in the parking lot today at lunchtime, I will ask you, please, if any parent comes to you with a concern, send them directly to the office. We want our school to be a community within our larger community, but we also want to keep our school community safe. I'm happy to answer any questions you may have in person.

Thank you
Lara Trujillo-Perez
Principal
Frederick Douglass International School

Great, that explained a whole lot of nothing. Maybe I should go to Lara and let her know what I found in Alonso's office?

I was still debating when my phone buzzed.

"Guesswhatguesswhatguesswhat?"

Cecilia tended to jump right into the conversation without a whole lot of preamble.

"I hope you're going to tell me?"

She squealed in a very un-Cecilia-like way. "I'm flying to Barcelona with Felip tomorrow! It's his mother's birthday this weekend and we're coming to surprise her."

"That's great! Will you have time to meet up or anything? I don't have a car—"

"We want you to come to the vineyard for dinner with us. On Saturday. You don't have plans, do you?"

"No, and I'd love to come with you," I said, my heart feeling a little lighter now that I knew I'd see my good friend. Maybe I could have some time alone with her and tell her about Alonso and ask her what I should do. She helped me find a new purpose with this job, maybe she could help me figure out what to do about him.

FIVE

4:05 PM Friday Frederick Douglass International School, Castelldefels, Catalonia, Spain

Friday afternoon came along and I was dreading another interaction with Paulo Ferrer, only it was after four and no one had arrived to pick up Pere.

"Hey, buddy, do you know who was supposed to pick you up today?"

Pere had been continuing to practice his piano piece, which he was actually picking up really quickly. The kid was so musically talented. Genes ran strong in that family.

"No, senyor Sutter," he said. "Mi papa is supposed to pick me up on Fridays but I know he has meetings sometimes."

"Meetings? You mean about his music business?"

Pere shrugged. "Sometimes. But he also meets with people about the separation."

Aw, the poor kid. He shouldn't have to worry about that kind of adult stuff. "Things are pretty rough at home, huh?"

"At home? No. Well, my stepmother doesn't like me very

much, but no. They are happy. No, the people meet him to talk about la independencia."

Footsteps echoed in the hallway outside.

"Oh, Pere, there you are. Thank you, Mr. Sutter. Pere's father called. He's running a bit late, so Pere, why don't you come with me to the office?"

"It's no trouble," I said. "I can stay with him. We've got practicing to do."

Lara smiled. "Thank you, Randall. See you at Bar Elena?"

"Yes, ma'am."

She gave a finger wave and was out the door, leaving me and Pere to hang out until his father arrived. I was tempted to ask him more questions, maybe figure out what was going on with his father, when I heard the squeak of wheels outside my door.

Alonso, dressed in his usual coveralls and cap, entered the room, his gaze darting toward Pere before he trained it on his current target. My garbage can.

"Senyor Sutter, are you married?"

I spun around to face Pere and laughed.

"Me? Married? No, Pere. Why do you ask?"

The little guy shrugged and shook his head. "I don't know. I just thought that if you were married, you probably would never ignore them if your new partner had a child."

My heart was breaking for this poor kid.

"No way, Pere. But sometimes..." *Shit.* Who was I to give out life advice? Oh, that was right. A teacher. *Dammit, Cecilia!* I was no good at this stuff! I hadn't even had a real long-term relationship, not unless you count the year I'd spent having sex with Rig. Which I didn't.

"Sometimes?"

Pere's lovely brown eyes grew round and shiny waiting for me to answer, and Alonso was puttering around now with a broom, although who the hell knew what he was actually sweeping.

"Sometimes people get so focused on one thing that they forget about what's important. That doesn't mean the important things are any *less* important. It just means that the person needs a reminder, right?" *And hopefully nothing bad happens in the meantime.* "It's like...do you play video games, Pere?"

He nodded. "When I'm allowed to, yes. I like them very much."

"You said when you're allowed to, that means someone is reminding you that school is most important right now, does that make sense? Because if you had no one to remind you, you might play only video games. Sometimes the shiny new thing becomes more important, and we need someone to remind us of our goals and what we have to do to reach them."

He frowned as he thought about it. "I see." Then he looked down again. "I wish someone would remind mi papa."

Oh, this kid. How could anyone...but then I knew my own family felt like I put my music before them. Maybe when you didn't share that important thing, it made it harder? Or maybe Mr. Ferrer was just an asshole who didn't pay attention to his son. That was always possible. He sure was missing out. Pere was such a great kid.

Maybe I'd be the one to remind his father—

"Pere, vine aquí. Come now, please hurry."

"Bona tarda, senyor Ferrer," I said, practicing my newly learned Catalan.

He grinned. "Rock Star. Com estàs?"

I smiled, fully aware that I should know that but I was still practicing on my app.

"Good. Pere has been working really hard on his—"

"Wonderful. Listen, I am having some people over in a week

or so. Perhaps you can come and accompany Pere. He wants to show what he is learning for his family."

I stood a little taller. "I'm...not sure. I would have to—"

"¿Señor Sutter?"

Alonso gestured for me to join him at my desk.

"Oh, excuse me. Ah, Mr. Ferrer? Your ID?"

His friendly banter ended as he pulled his wallet out and jammed his ID under the scanner, then called to Pere in Catalan and spoke to him in a gruff manner until Pere reached him in the hallway. Pere looked back once and waved before his father yanked him forward.

I turned and cursed, walking toward Alonso.

"Are you going to go? To his house?"

"Are we speaking now?"

He met my gaze as we stood two feet away from each other, close enough to remember what it was like to be even closer.

"Randall—"

"Why?"

"Why what?"

I exhaled. "Are you really going to make me ask all the whys?"

He put his hands on his hips, peeked around me, then held up a finger. He trotted over to the door, looked into the hallway, then closed the door. He walked back my way...and took my fucking breath away. My whole body was vibrating, wanting... something intense from this exchange but was also hopping mad that I still felt this way even though he'd ignored me for weeks.

He stood closer to me and he reached for my forearm. "Randall, you need to stay away from Paolo Ferrer."

I narrowed my eyes and pulled my arm away from him, causing him to take a step back. "Why are you so interested in the Ferrers?"

He sighed and his hands planted back on his hips, which

even in his shapeless coveralls turned me into one of Pavlov's dogs.

"I can't tell you," he said in a voice barely above a whisper. "But I want you to be safe."

His words chilled me. "Is Pere safe? God, I knew I should have talked to Lara. I'm worried about him—"

"She knows."

"Okay."

We were quiet, standing before each other, and inside I was screaming. *Why? Why? Why? All the why. Why avoid me? Why pretend you don't speak English? Why—*

"I want to answer your whys. I can't. Not now. But I will."

"You will? You mean you'll talk to me?"

He looked at his feet and shook his head. "Randall...it is hard."

I couldn't help it. I snorted.

"What?"

"I hope so."

It was the absolute wrong thing to say, but then that slight curve of his lips returned. "You *know* so."

I couldn't breathe. "What now?"

He stepped back. "You go to Bar Elena with the others." He continued backing toward the door.

"Are you coming?"

"No."

And I deflated. I started to speak and he held up a hand as he reached the door.

"The whys. I will answer them. Soon."

"Alonso?"

"Sí?"

What else could I say? Had we made progress? Was I still mad? I was so turned around—and turned on—I was ready to thank this guy for not speaking to me and worrying about my safety and pretending like he didn't speak English. Instead, I stood there staring. Speechless.

"Si us plau. No et preocupis."

"I know I should know what that means."

"And do you know?" He winked at me. And left.

What the fuck was I supposed to do with that? I really needed to learn Catalan más rápido. While I was still learning Spanish. And a new job.

Lara and Madame Lahlou were not at Bar Elena when I arrived, but the rest of the staff was chattering away.

"Oh, Randall. So glad you are here. Sit beside me," Josette said, immediately getting me settled and going to the bar to get me a glass of wine. I was still a little dazed and happy to have her fussing tonight.

"Are you feeling all right?" Camille asked me.

I gave a half shrug. "Yeah, just a weird afternoon." But then my gaze landed on a TV set in the corner, and though I couldn't follow the story, I recognized the subject.

Images of a protest, very similar to the one I'd been caught in, flashed on the screen, the familiar flag. Josette returned with my wine and I put a hand on her arm.

"Do you know what that's all about?"

She followed my gaze. "Oh, the separatist movement?" When I nodded, she leaned closer and spoke quietly in my ear. "Oui. There is a large faction of people in Catalonia who want to not only be an autonomous region, but separate from Spain. In two thousand seventeen there was a crisis, the people voted on whether or not to have an independence vote, but it was illegal. Members of the Catalan European Democratic Party went to prison, some fled the country."

And then a man's face appeared on the screen, and I jerked in my seat.

"I've seen him," I said, grabbing her arm. "In the parking lot, with Mr. Ferrer."

Her eyes widened and she squinted at the screen, but then his picture was gone.

"Be sure to let Lara know. Probably it's nothing, but you never know."

I nodded and thanked her. She went back to the conversation but I continued to sip my wine and watch the TV screen until someone switched it to a fútbol match, which made even less sense to me. I hadn't been a big sports guy growing up, never played, never watched, so the fact that this country was borderline obsessive about fútbol meant that I did a lot of smiling and nodding when people talked to me about it and asked me which team I followed.

I walked back to my apartment with my French ladies and was still replaying my conversation with Alonso in my head, so I missed Sasha's question.

"Hola Randall? You are okay?"

"Yes, I'm sorry. Just been a strange day." *Week. Month. Year.*

"We wanted to know if you would go with us into Barcelona tomorrow? We want to rent bikes and ride around."

"Oh, thank you, but I'm not sure I'm ready for that after my crash," I said with my hands out. "Also, my old teacher from California is flying in with her fiancé, and I'm having dinner with them at his family's winery."

Their eyes widened and they cooed over that news. "That sounds lovely. You will have a wonderful time. Bring us back some good wine, oui?"

"Of course," I said, "and you have a great time. Be careful," I said, thinking of the last time I was out and about in Barcelona. The protest. Alonso. My life-changing experience.

And as I climbed the steps to my apartment and closed the door behind me, I had another life-altering thought.

I had no idea what to wear to a surprise birthday family dinner at a winery, no idea where to even shop for something to wear to a winery, nor how to behave at one.

Despite living close to wine country in California, drinking wine and visiting wineries was not something I was raised with, and becoming what everyone else thought of as a rock star, and which I referred to as my job as a professional musician, wine drinking and wineries wasn't part of all that.

My father worked for one of the largest lumber companies near Grass Valley, California, and my mother was a preschool teacher. My three brothers were all firefighters with Cal Fire, and my sister worked at the preschool with my mother as they were very close. I was the black sheep in all manner of speaking in my family, the one who had shirked my hard-working, blue-collar responsibilities to chase a dream, as my father would say. And even when our debut album charted, and then our next record went gold, and then our third album got over a million streams in the first week...my father wasn't satisfied.

When I mentioned to my oldest brother, Mark, that I'd made more money than our father would in a decade working for the lumberyard, and why couldn't he respect that, it got back to my father. And he very calmly told me that since I thought I was so much better than him, I could feel free to uninvite myself to their house for Christmas last year.

I hadn't seen my family since, though I did check in with my mother and sister and let them know I was alive from time to time. Mom assured me that while I was justified to feel hurt by my father's constant criticism, I needed to apologize and make things right. I didn't agree, though I knew that I would have to eventually suck it up if I wanted to see at least my mom and sister.

My next-oldest brother, Dustin, was even more of a blowhard than our father, and after him came the youngest son, Matt, who tried to play peacemaker but always sided with the other two. Mayra, my sister, was the baby and she could never understand why all the drama? It seemed to me that without me present, there *was* no drama, and so maybe that was the best gift I could give my family. My absence.

And all of this family drama thinking wasn't going to help me with tomorrow. At least Cecilia would be there. I could watch her to know which utensil to use. I'd met Felip when he moved to California over the summer. They came to see our last show in LA before we headed to Europe. He was an outgoing, gregarious man who was absolutely enamored with Cecilia, which made him a good guy in my book.

I wished I had a guitar to bang around on, as my mind was spinning and playing music was often the only way I had to come down after a day like I'd had, but since I hadn't gotten around to getting a new one, I did the other thing that helped, although it also made me think more...and in this case, swoon.

Yeah. I wrote about Alonso. Remembering every detailed from how he smelled, to how he sounded when he was being all evasive, what his answers would be to my whys.

By the time I felt I'd purged enough, I knew three things:

1. I needed a guitar
2. I needed a new notebook
3. I needed all of his whys

SIX

I'd breathed a sigh of relief when Cecilia and Felip picked me up dressed in jeans and sweaters. Cecilia was also wearing Chucks, as was I, with my nicest jeans (read: no holes) and my favorite cardigan.

I'm not sure why it ranked my favorite other than it was charcoal gray, had maroon stripes around the left arm, it went with everything, and it was soft. I wasn't even sure of the fabric it was made out of, as I'd ripped the tag off years ago. I did that with all of my clothes because I had a thing about textures. As a kid I was forced to wear whatever my brothers handed down. Nothing ever fit right, but I never complained, just dealt with the itchy-scratchy show. As an adult, I found the softest, most comfortable clothes, and that's what I lived in. Thankfully, in my genre of music there wasn't a dress code, and since cardigans were the most utilitarian and comfortable of outerwear options

—and they tended to hide unflattering bits—they became my thing. I wore them until they disintegrated.

"I hope my cousin is keeping this place maintained well," Felip said, shaking my hand at the door to my apartment. "You let me know if I need to talk to him."

Cecilia took me in her arms and groaned at Felip.

"You're only looking for a reason to mess with him and you know it." She squeezed me a good long time. "Are you okay?" she asked me, her tone serious.

"Yeah, I am, actually," I said, smiling at her, so glad to be back in her orbit. Cecilia was just one of those people who had the right sense of humor to bring you out of any blue mood and have you in stitches. As a teacher, her class had always been my favorite, first in Life Skills as a freshman, which I'd liked so much, I'd taken three years of American Sign Language with her. That sign language came in handy now as she signed, *Are you sure you're okay? You'd tell me?*

I signed back, *It's been a ride, but the job is great, thank you for your help, and so far I really like living here. You can say you told me so because I really like teaching. Anything else going on will have to wait until later to discuss.*

"Hey, hey, now, if you two keep that up I'm going to speak Catalan all night."

Cecilia poked his side and he signed to her, *Mean teacher.*

"I'm actually trying to learn," I said, "so I wouldn't mind. I'm also trying to learn more about Catalonia."

Felip gave me a big smile. "Well, you're in for a treat. Papa will love to talk about all things Catalunya. He is a bit of a history buff."

Cecilia met Felip on the flight over to Spain back in June, with students from my old high school. She got roped into chaperoning when her good friend and my second favorite teacher,

Ms. Reyes, was injured in a car accident right before the school tour was about to take place.

"Señor Segura is one of my favorite people, Randall, you will love him. He has the best energy."

"I'm sure I will. Who else will be there? And this is a surprise for your mother, right Mr. Segura?"

"Por favor, call me Felip. I can't get used to Cecilia's students calling me Mr. Segura. That's only my father, and I'm not that old."

Cecilia laughed. "Well, you're sorta old."

That made me burst out laughing. Cecilia wasn't old, nor would she probably ever act old. I had no idea how old Felip was, but he had such joie de vivre that I was sure even when he *was* old, he'd probably still be fun.

"You wound me, woman. Just because I have turned forty."

She ruffled his hair and then stopped to closely, comically, examine him for gray hair, of which he had a healthy amount.

She whispered something in his ear, he growled, she kissed him, and I was beginning to have second thoughts. Did I really have the fortitude to be around lovebirds all night?

"Two of my brothers I know for sure will be there. I have not heard from my other brother, as he sometimes disappears for weeks without letting us know what he's doing. Also, our COO, June Fontaine, will be there. She was my second and now she is running my youngest brother ragged." He chuckled. "I'm not so secretly glad it's not me."

Cecilia rolled her eyes. "June has a tough job wrangling you Seguras. You should give her a break. And a raise."

Something had just become very clear to me. "Um, so, I hadn't put it together until right now but holy shit, you're *Segura* Segura? I've had your wine!"

Felip did a little wiggle dance and clapped his hands

together. "And? What did you think? Which kind did you have? Dime más, por favor."

Cecilia grabbed my hand. "Darling, he will tell you all about it in the car, but if we don't leave now, we're going to be late for the surprise."

Felip put his arm around me. "Sure, sure. You are ready? You need anything? Oh, bé, you tell me what you think about my wine, and then I will tell you all about how I came to be infatuated with your music."

I gave a nervous chuckle as they swept me out the door of my apartment and into Felip's waiting Audi. He grilled me during the drive on what wine I'd had, and like the uncultured wine person I was, all I could tell him was that I'd had a cabernet sauvignon at, um, a friend's house, and that I bought a bottle at the store by my apartment. That was not enough information for him, and he asked me what I thought, what wine I typically drank, and I decided I should come clean.

"Felip, I'm sorry, but I've exhausted my wine knowledge. I only know that I've had it, I liked it enough to buy a bottle, which I've managed to nearly finish, and that I will most likely order it again at the bar."

Cecilia turned around and high-fived me. "Thank you. You have no idea how frustrated he gets with me and my non-wine-drinking self. At least you liked it, though."

"Cariño, you know I love to watch the faces you make when you try the new wines, and bless you for being a good sport. Someday we'll find one you hate less."

We all laughed at that and I took a moment to look around at the changing scenery. We'd left the city of Castelldefels and were in a wooded area at the base of the hills surrounding Barcelona proper when I noticed the Audi beginning to climb.

"Ah, I missed this car," Felip said, and Cecilia pouted at him.

"I'm sorry. I know I've kept you from your beloved car, and country, and family for that matter—"

"No, no no no, cariño." He laced his fingers with hers and kissed her hand. "I am perfectly happy with you in California. And we have been back here three times now since I left a year and a half ago. I'm having the time of my life, I promise."

Cecilia looked at him with so much love in her gaze, I felt guilty intruding on their moment. Until she turned on me.

"So you've told me you're okay, and I want to hear more about what it's like working at Frederick Douglass, but you haven't mentioned whether you've met anyone interesting." She turned in her seat and waggled her eyebrows at me.

I sighed. I wasn't sure I wanted to unload my tale of woe—or *whoa* in this case—in front of Felip.

"I did, before I left Barcelona. It was fun, but now I'm focused on the job and I've made some really great friends." I told them about my French gal pals, about my cool boss, and Ivan and our shared love of music. I hoped that would take the attention off of my bachelor status.

Cecilia gazed at me between the seats. "I'm so happy to hear it. I swear I'm trying so hard not to say I told you so—"

"You're allowed to say it," I said, and Felip laughed.

"She's always right," he said, and then hissed as she pinched his side. "Senyora, we are on a very dangerous mountain road and I must concentrate."

She turned back to me. "Well, once you get more settled in, you'll meet someone, probably when you least expect it. I just hope when it happens he absolutely sweeps you off of your feet. You deserve that after all that has happened."

"Thanks," I said, though I wasn't sure I wanted to go there. I had tamped that rejection and hurt from my band and from Rig down deep and kept it buried in order to keep moving forward. My confidence had surely taken a hit, though. So many years of being afraid of people's motives in getting involved with me and then having those fears come to fruition? I knew it was a mistake to get involved with Rig from the get-go, but I hadn't trusted myself to do what was best for me yet.

Maybe that was why I was so unsettled about Alonso. Not only was he involved in something that worried me, but could I trust that he wouldn't disappear again? Could I trust *anything* he'd said?

We pulled into the driveway as the last rays of sunlight filtered through a grove of citrus trees alongside the path, with a gorgeous house set back from the winery complex. It was all very quaint and old. Very old. Stone and white plaster. I wondered just how many years this place had been here, how long Felip's family had been making wine?

Felip pulled the Audi around behind the main house and parked out of sight next to a Mercedes and a Toyota pickup.

"Papa wants us to meet in the winery's dining room, so Mama won't stress about cleaning up after us bad kids."

"She had four boys," Cecilia said. "What did she think was going to happen?"

We left the car and walked along a lighted path past the house and into one of the buildings with a rounded roof. Inside, it looked even more ancient but with tables and candles and photographs along the walls that seemed to range in eras.

"Ah, bé, you made it!"

An older man moved toward Cecilia with his arms out and picked her up in a big hug, then he hugged Felip and pounded on his back. There were cheek kisses. And then he turned to me.

"¿Qui és?" He held his hand out for me and I shook it, my hand trembling a bit.

"Jo sóc Randall Sutter."

His eyes brightened in surprise, and he turned on Cecilia. "And he's been practicing his Catalan, unlike someone I know."

She laughed, and I figured this was a long-running joke between them. Then she began to sign to me. *This is Mr. Segura and he is a wonderful man. You will love him, though be prepared, he will very likely pull out his guitar once he knows you are a musician. He and Felip play sometimes. I love it but it gets competitive.*

"This is how it's going to be, huh?" Mr. Segura said to Felip, who shrugged but then winked at me.

"Thanks for the warning," I said out loud as I signed back to her. Cecilia was hard of hearing, but she wore hearing aids and you'd honestly never know unless she didn't have them in for some reason. She could pick up the quietest conversations in the back of the room, or when kids would try to cheat. If ever a teacher had eyes in the back of their head, and super-hearing, it was her.

"Why are you warning people, eh, senyora?"

Another man came forward, this one looking very much like Felip.

"Randall, this is my brother Tomás, and over there with the lovely harpy—I mean enchanting woman—"

"Felip, I swear," the woman said, exasperated. I was surprised that she had an American accent. I'd assumed she'd be Spanish if she worked with the Seguras. She pushed back from the table with a huff, exchanged a look with the young man who seemed not much older than me, and they both approached us.

"My youngest brother, Mateu, and June, my dearest friend and the person fully capable of eviscerating me—I mean, running Cava Segura."

"Pleased to meet you," June said. "I'm really a professional babysitter and cleaner."

"Sí, like Harvey Keitel in *Pulp Fiction*," Tomás said, and she rolled her eyes.

"Mucho gusto," Mateu said quietly as he shook my hand. "I promise we are not all obnoxious."

"Who's obnoxious?" Felip put his arms around his similarly handsome brothers, and I could absolutely see the worry about cleaning up messes.

"Now, everyone to your places. My beautiful wife will be arriving any moment."

Mr. Segura shooed us over to a table that was set with all the fancy shit that I was afraid of using. He sat at the head of the table, Felip sat at the other end with Cecilia at his right hand. And, much to my chagrin, I was seated across from her with a seat left empty on one side of me. Tomás sat next to Cecilia, June sat next to me with Mateu on her other side, next to his father. Great, the most intimidating person was next to me.

"Don't worry," she said, leaning in. "Once they start talking, no one pays any attention to etiquette. They are very neat and proper, but eating with the Seguras is like any old family dinner."

I turned sharply toward her, and she raised her eyebrow and winked at me.

Perhaps not so scary.

"You haven't been to a Sutter family meal. I swear the food gets cold from the icy glares my father gives to whoever is on his bad side that day."

She elbowed me. "Then you've come to the right place to have a good time." She gazed at the gathered folks with a fond smile.

Those gathered continued to whisper quietly until they heard the front doors open and the scolding of an older woman in Catalan. Everyone froze as we heard two sets of footsteps coming toward us, the arguing voices growing louder until they turned the corner.

As a group, we shouted, "Happy Birthday!"

Mrs. Segura clutched at her chest, her eyes wide, and she fell against the man escorting her.

With a familiar chin dimple.

I lifted my hands to clap along with everyone but I couldn't make them work.

The protest, the school, and now here?

What. The. Hell?

"Ay, fill meu! You grace us with your presence!"

Alonso made his way to his father's side, held out his hand to shake, and the old man pulled him in for a tight embrace, speaking in his ear for several moments before he let him go with a stern expression on his face.

Alonso gave him a curt nod, and then he stopped to hug and kiss Mateu, then June, passed me by as I tried not to swallow my own tongue or faint or something ridiculous like that on his way to Felip.

"Germà, it's been a long time."

Felip hugged his brother Alonso just as their father had, speaking to him in his ear, but with Felip, he grew annoyed and pulled away, nodding and waving his words away. He went for Cecilia and gave her a big hug, lifting her off the ground. She laughed heartily, and then when he set her down, she held out her hand to gesture to me.

And *he* looked as if he'd swallowed his tongue.

"Alonso, this is my former student, Randall Sutter. He's working at the Frederick Douglass International School now in Castelldefels."

The empty seat next to me was meant for him, and he watched me carefully, no trace of a smile on his face as he took the seat, held out his hand to shake, and then turned to look down at his plate as the conversation grew in volume.

I was sure he could hear my heartbeat over it all.

I broke out in a sweat beneath my cardigan and dress shirt.

We had a fair amount of distance between us but his thigh brushed mine and we both jolted at the contact.

The meal was served—steak and a vegetable dish called escalivada, along with bread and a few other small plates—and June had been right. The men barely paid attention to the food as they continued to chat in a mixture of English, Spanish, and Catalan. It was quite civilized, however Felip sloshed wine out of his glass with his enthusiastic hand gestures.

Alonso and I both moved to cut our steak at the same time and we bumped elbows. I hadn't noticed before that he was left-handed. He gave me a quick look while keeping his head down, and he ate swiftly and efficiently, as if he thought he might be able to sneak away without having to answer any questions.

No. Way.

This was one too many coincidences.

"Glad you made it," Felip said to him, putting a hand on his forearm. "You've been out of contact for a while. Everything okay?"

Alonso shrugged. "You know how it is." He glanced in their father's direction and then shrugged again. I had an inkling I knew what it was about.

It sure seemed like Alonso and I shared a place in our family's hierarchy.

It was weird being served by the winery staff but I understood that they were handling the festivities to give Mrs. Segura a break for her birthday. They offered us flights of wine, and I looked to Felip to tell me about each one. Cecilia made faces at it all, every single one she tried, and I cracked up, almost forgetting the elephant in the room of *what the ever-*

loving fuck was my savior—Alonso *Segura*, apparently—doing here?

After the meal came a decadent chocolate cake. It was sincerely the best food I'd had since I'd been in Spain, and the wine had me feeling kind of floaty. When we were fully sated, and I was ready for a nap, Cecilia put me on the spot.

"Senyor Segura? Do you know that Randall is actually quite an accomplished musician?"

"Filla, call me Papa. You know better."

Cecilia blushed and nodded. "It's true. Randall was here on tour with his band from America and he decided to finally heed his calling as a teacher and stay a while."

"They're really quite good," Felip said. "They've played all over the world, and even on BBC and Telecinco."

Mr. Segura rubbed his hands together. "Then we must go up to the house. Since my eldest son moved away and doesn't play guitar with me anymore, you will play with me."

Felip groaned as he pushed back from the table. Everyone else started to get up, with the exception of June and Mateu, who excused themselves to help the staff clean up after the meal. I pushed my chair back, preoccupied, thinking about playing music for this man, when I stumbled and the sleeve of my sweater caught on my chair, tearing one of the small holes into a cavern.

"Aw, man." I deflated. I didn't want to be finished with my favorite sweater.

Alonso grabbed my elbow, and I flinched.

"Are you okay?" he asked, low so only I would hear him.

"Not really, no."

He pulled back, still holding my arm, and placed his other arm around my back. "What do you need?"

I narrowed my eyes at him. "The. Whys."

He nodded and looked down. "Later. I promise. Just please,

don't say anything to my family, not until I have a chance to explain."

I pulled away from him and straightened my clothes, feeling silly with a gaping hole in my sleeve. I frowned at him, but of course I would do as he asked. I didn't want to upset these nice people, but I damn sure didn't want my friend Cecilia in the middle of something dangerous. He better have a good fucking explanation for everything.

SEVEN

SATURDAY 9:08 PM Cava Segura Winery, Pènedes, Catalonia, Spain

The Segura house was lovely and much homier than the winery's fancy dining room. It felt like an appropriate abode for a family with four sons, sons that ran around inside even if they knew they shouldn't, who wrestled, argued, but who banded together when it counted.

From what I learned tonight, that was exactly what it was like. Cecilia told me on the walk over that the brothers were close, but Alonso hadn't been around much and Felip had been worried about him.

No shit.

"I was an only child so it took a bit for me to understand their bickering. Now I get it. I feel like I'll be getting three brothers when we get married."

"And when will that be?" I asked her.

She held a finger to her lips and pointed for us to get inside the house.

The living room had three big couches and two chairs. Mr. Segura gestured for me to take one of the latter and he handed me an acoustic guitar.

"You play, huh?"

I smiled. "Not flamenco, I'm afraid, but guitar, yes. Since I was twelve."

He took the chair closest to me and gestured for me to play something.

Carefully, I adjusted the tuning, loving the way the strings felt under my fingertips. I felt so emotional, having a guitar in my hands again after everything that happened, I had to just breathe for a moment, afraid I would cry in front of all these people.

I blew out a breath and looked to Cecilia for strength.

"Oh! Play 'My Heart' would you? That's my favorite one."

Everyone was staring. Mrs. Segura stood beside her husband, her hands on his shoulders. She leaned down to kiss him and then asked if anyone wanted coffee or tea. Mateu had just come in with June and he went to go help her.

I began to play the first song I ever wrote, the one that I recorded on the four-track that I bought with the money from my first job at a pizza joint in Grass Valley. The song made it onto our first album and was even one of the singles that made it onto radio. Satellite radio played it on their hits station and it went viral when some kids did a dance challenge to it on social media.

I was too nervous and emotional to sing, and I didn't trust myself, but then Cecilia signed to me to sing. I groaned a little and then gave in.

Mr. Segura smiled the whole time, as did Felip, with Cecilia in front of him on the couch clapping along. Tomás began to sing along and snap his fingers, and when June and Mateu came back, she gasped and then spoke excitedly to him, as if she just realized that she knew my music.

Alonso stood behind the couch with his arms crossed over his chest, watching me intently, which might have thrown me, but performing was the one place I didn't tend to doubt myself. Before I started? Absolutely. I'd had epic bouts with stage fright from time to time. Once I put fingers to strings, keys, or whatever I was playing, the world fell away and I knew that I was where I was supposed to be. I wasn't a hugely demonstrative front man, though I knew how to work a crowd now that I'd been doing this a long time. But when I was off stage? Then doubts and wonderings crept in.

So when I finished the song, and the whole room erupted in cheers, my gaze lingered on Alonso, who didn't clap.

But he smiled. A full smile. With teeth.

"I can't believe it! I love that song. I never thought...I mean, you never think you're going to meet someone in real life that sings one of your favorite songs, right?" Tomás shook his head. "That's so cool."

"And now you teach music to children?" asked Mr. Segura.

There it was. The big question.

"I do. When I was in high school, Cecilia encouraged me to become a teacher, so I went to Cal Berkeley for my music degree and teaching credential—"

"Go Bears," Felip said, but he covered his mouth and gestured for me to go on.

"I forgot. Cecilia told me you went to Berkeley. That's cool. Anyway, yeah, I wanted to do the whole musician thing. It worked out...for a while. Until it didn't. I loved it. And now I'm giving teaching a try."

"But MoonCraft is great! Are you done performing?" Tomás asked.

I shrugged and ran my fingers lovingly over Mr. Segura's

guitar. I took one of the cloth napkins that Mrs. Segura had out on the table for the snacks she'd brought out and I rubbed down the neck, not wanting to leave any oils on what appeared to be a very old guitar. I handed it back to him and his smile was warm and genuine. I hated to let it go.

"The band is done. I'm not sure what's in my future. I'm… regrouping."

"Yeah, because his instruments and belongings were stolen in Barcelona," Felip said, shaking his head. "It is terrible. Are things so bad in Barcelona?"

Mr. Segura muttered something in Catalan. "Perhaps if people were more concerned about safety and less about this foolhardy independence pursuit." He shook his head.

Alonso turned sharply to look at his father. "Papa—"

Mr. Segura spoke gruffly to him in Catalan, and Felip frowned.

"Papa Segura? Can you please explain?" Cecilia asked him. "Randall and I were talking about this earlier, and I don't have a good understanding of the separatists' stance."

Alonso's face seemed to go a little pale. He once more pleaded with his father in Catalan, which Mr. Segura ignored.

"Catalunya has an independent spirit. There is a lot of history going back hundreds of years of conflict with Madrid, but in recent times, both after the civil war in 1979 and in 2010, we have been given autonomy, only to have pieces of it be taken back before all of the aspects could be implemented. A lot of people are frustrated. Pero, splitting with Madrid will most likely be bad for our economy as it will threaten all of our agreements with the European Union. Brexit was a perfect example of how wrong things can go."

"But Papa," Felip interjected. "When they held the referendum in twenty-seventeen, didn't it pass with a resounding majority?"

"It was a vote to have a vote, fill. And only forty-three percent of the eligible voters actually turned up, so that is not a mandate by any means."

I almost raised my hand. I think Cecilia caught me too. "But, sir? What would be the reasons to become independent? Or not to?"

"People want to protect what is Catalunya, verdad?" Tomás said. "Our language and culture are unique, and there was a long part of history where the central government wanted to wipe out all that was Catalan. Children were not taught our language, it was forbidden to be spoken in public. With the nationalist movements going on in the world, who is to say they would not try again?"

"It all comes down to money," Mr. Segura said. "We have it, Madrid wants to be able to use it."

"It is the principle of the matter," Mateu said. "The Spanish government says 'no, you can't vote,' and the people, they don't want to be told no."

Felip sighed. "Of course we want to be respected and given our autonomy, but there are benefits to all of Spain for us to remain, to the European Union as well. I feel for Scotland. I know they did not want Brexit."

Alonso remained quiet during the conversation, though his frown told me he might have strong feelings, one way or another.

"Enough of politics," Mr. Segura said, grabbing his wine glass and refilling it before making his way around the room with the bottle, filling everyone's glass despite protests. I was feeling incredibly warm and sleepy and happy to be surrounded by such wonderful, generous, intelligent people. My family would never have sat around discussing politics and history.

"If you don't mind, Papa," Felip said. "I do have one more bit of the dramatic."

His tone was enough to startle his father, who sloshed a bit of wine onto the table. Alonso was there with a towel to clean up the mess and check on his father.

"Ves amb compte, germà," Alonso said, giving a warning to his brother.

"Si us plau, Papa. It's only that Cecilia and I want to ask your blessing to have our nuptials here at the winery in June."

The room fell silent for the briefest of moments before everyone erupted in cheers. Mr. Segura pounded on Felip's back and kissed him on the lips, squeezing his face, then shoved him toward Mrs. Segura, who was crying and laughing. Mr. Segura squeezed Cecilia tight as she wiped tears from her eyes. Happy tears.

More wine was spilled as hugs went around. I sat back and waited until Cecilia was free to give her a hug. I didn't want to intrude on what was obviously a big moment for Felip's family.

But then Felip pulled me up and hugged me, then passed me over to Cecilia, who held me tight, her body trembling.

"Congratulations," I whispered to her.

"Thanks." She pulled back and grinned. "I knew they'd be happy, but I wasn't expecting all this!"

Mr. Segura picked up his guitar and began to play a beautiful flamenco tune, and he sang in that kind of throaty, husky voice that I had always been fascinated by. The next thing I knew, Felip had a guitar and the two played and sang together, while Mateu and Tomás clapped along with their mother.

I looked around for Alonso and spotted him through the dining room to the kitchen. He was doing the dishes. I wanted to get up and help him but I was riveted by the music being made before me. I was sure I could be forgiven as the musician inside me was in heaven, so honored to be a part of such an important family moment.

But then nature called.

Which gave me a perfect opportunity to find Alonso and demand some answers.

Only, I got distracted going to the bathroom, transfixed by the many family pictures lining the walls of the hallway of the old house. I finally found what I needed, did my business, and took a look at myself as I washed my hands. I'd left my hair down tonight, which I normally didn't do, but the unpredictable brown and reddish-blond streaked waves were actually quite calm today, and it had reached a length finally where it would remain behind my shoulders when I ate or did some other activity where I needed it out of the way.

My cheeks were rosy from all the wine and my eyelids were heavy. I looked thoroughly sauced, and while I felt safe and in control of my faculties, I realized that everyone had been drinking, including Felip and Cecilia, and we were quite far from Castelldefels. Did Cabify or Uber even come out this far?

I heard a tap on the door, and I realized I'd been gone for some time and I still wanted to give Alonso a piece of my mind, drunk or not. Only, when I flung the door open and found Alonso's concerned expression, I lost my fight a little. Until he opened his mouth.

"Were you sick?"

For some reason that made me quite indignant.

"I was not, thank you. I'm not that messy of a drunk."

"You certainly wouldn't be the first of us or our guests to be sick in that bathroom after a night like tonight."

The lift at the corner of his lips had once enticed me, but right now I was...sassy, apparently.

"Why are you lurking out here in the hallway?"

He backed up to give me space to leave the bathroom if I chose, but I wanted answers. Whys. I wanted them *now*. Dammit.

"I know you have questions. I appreciate you not asking in front of my family."

"But you're still not going to tell me."

He sighed, glanced toward the living room where the guitars had gone quiet, but there was still a lot of happily boisterous discussion. Alonso held his hand out to me. "Come. Let's go for a walk."

I stared at his hand for a moment, which was foolish, because I knew I'd take it and follow him wherever he led me, whether it was good for me or not. I wanted answers more than security.

His grip was warm and firm as he led me farther down the hallway away from the family room. We went through a sort of mudroom and out onto a back step, where the hillside was bathed in moonlight.

"It's very beautiful here," I said, needing to acknowledge that fact. I'd been so nervous and overwhelmed when we arrived that I hadn't had the words, but the drive up had been breathtaking.

"To me it is the most beautiful place on Earth," he said, and I melted at his words. He didn't let go of my hand once we took the path leading into the vineyard and away from the house.

I couldn't stop smiling.

"Where I grew up? Grass Valley? It's picturesque there, too, but I didn't grow up around...well, anything as wonderful as your family. Your parents, everyone was so nice to me, so welcoming." And obviously my tongue was relaxed.

"What happened to Alonso, is what you're thinking."

"No!" I was mortified. Had I intimated that?

But he chuckled, keeping his gaze forward. "They are wonderful people, but it is not easy to go against their wishes."

"And you have?" Now we were getting somewhere. I didn't

want to push him, but then again, he wouldn't have brought me out here if he didn't want to talk.

He slowed down as we reached a plateau that opened to a vista that was incredible.

"Whoa," I breathed. "And you grew up here?"

"Sí. Cava Segura has been in our family for five generations. My grandparents still lived here when I was small. My father had already taken over the business, but it is as it is now for Felip—well, Mateu, now that Felip is in California." He exhaled. "Mateu was running the California operation but there were some problems and he wanted to be home. It just so happened that Felip met his little teacher and fell in love, so it worked out perfect."

His expression didn't match what he'd said.

"And Tomás? He lives in Madrid?"

"Sí. Papa knew he had instilled the travel bug in Tomás, so when he announced he wanted to start his own company doing tours throughout the country, Felip backed him and our father reluctantly agreed."

"Forgive me if I'm confused that your family runs this successful winery and you...work at the school?"

He looked down, shaking his head. "This is the part that I should not be telling you."

"What *can* you tell me, Alonso? Because from where I stand? We had what I thought was a great night, I left you my number, you never called, which—fine. I wasn't really surprised. But then I show up to Frederick Douglass and...and you...and you *lie*? You don't speak English? Come on, what am I supposed to think?"

He nodded and then turned to me, the whites of his eyes practically glowing around his deep brown irises. He squeezed my hand just enough to make a point.

"Why weren't you surprised that I didn't call you?"

"Wha— Well, I've had people blow me off plenty of times. That never surprises me. But none of them lied about speaking the same language to do it."

"They were ignorant to let you go. *I* was...ignorant."

"I'm sure you had your reasons for leaving me in the dark."

"Your poem was beautiful," he said, the corner of his lips turning up. "I keep it with me."

That admission stunned me. He was so many things, and sentimental was a welcome addition to what I knew of him. "There's more where that came from," I said. "You inspired me." I couldn't, wouldn't, admit my re-creation—Randall 2.0—was due to his challenging words.

"I hate that I've kept you in the dark." He huffed out a breath. "Randall, I can't talk about what I'm doing at the school. I can't tell you much. In my past, I can say that I did my required military service, and it suited me. Mama hated that I re-enlisted. I tried to appease my parents by contributing what I can to Cava Segura. I handle the technology and security needs, but I am not...free. ¿Me entiendes?"

His words hung in the night between us and understanding opened like the night-blooming flowers that ran up the trellises on the sides of the winery and the house.

"Are you...*intelligence*?" I whispered. "Like...you *can't* talk about it?"

His gaze was pleading, he wanted me to understand without him having to spell it out.

"It's not that you don't *want* to give me your whys?" I attempted to clarify without asking him too much.

"Sí, Randall. I want to give them *all* to you."

And under the moonlight on a hillside covered in what I understood to be some of the most valuable grapes in the world, Alonso placed his hand on my jaw and stepped closer to me.

"Know this little bit. I desperately wanted to call you, but that night we spent together was an indulgence that could have compromised everything. Can that be enough for you to trust me? For now? It's been killing me to see you every day, to keep everything from you when I just want to be with you, like this. I have never taken such a risk, never lost focus before, but I can't regret it. That night was...the first time I've felt like *me* since I signed my life over to someone else's discretion."

He seemed to lose the wind in his sails, so I wrapped my arms around his waist and held him to keep him from blowing away.

"How can I *not* accept that?"

He trembled and pressed our foreheads together. "My family doesn't know me. I tell them I am serving, I am gone, I will be out of contact for some time...Mama says I break her heart. Papa is angry with me for upsetting Mama. Felip is angry that I'm upsetting our parents, thinks I am being selfish. The other two are glad it's not them in my shoes. I'm trying to do what's right for not only my family, but my people...I know that sounds dramatic." He laughed then, but his trembling grew stronger under my hands.

"And then I come along with my whys."

He laughed again, but it came out more like a gasp. He caressed my jaw then and ran a thumb over my bottom lip. "Can you and your whys forgive me?"

"Forgiveness is the easy part," I said, running my hands up under his shirt, causing him to shiver. "The rest of the whys can wait. What I *don't* know about now is the hows."

"The hows?"

"Mmm. How am I supposed to act around you? How can I be here for you? *Can* I be here for you?" Then I laughed a little harder than I think he was expecting. "How do I get home since everyone in that house is wasted?"

That was the right thing to say, at least it seemed that way, as Alonso laughed with me, burying his face in my neck. I held him tight to me, but he held me tighter, and he took several deep breaths as though he were trying to put himself back together.

"Hows are easier than whys. How you act depends on what you want the others to know. How you act depends on whether or not you want to be the center of a Segura bomb like we saw tonight. My family doesn't do anything small...and I've never talked to them about who I see. They do not know that I am bisexual. They never ask, I don't offer."

"That's so sad, Alonso. I'd want them to be just as happy for you as they were for Felip and Cecilia in there."

"But Felip is the golden boy. Well, he was a little tarnished because he got divorced from his first wife and he has not given Mama grandbabies yet. Anything I do will be met first with frustration about how I never tell them anything, how I'm never around. After a while it was just easier to stay away."

"Is that what you want?"

He shrugged and pulled back to look into my eyes, to brush my hair out of my face.

"That is a separate issue. What I want is right here."

I broke out into a huge grin of triumph. "*That* is excellent."

He exhaled again. "Randall, what this means is that tonight we can forget whys and hows. But away from here, where we are not safe from prying eyes, we have to go back to not knowing each other, to me being Alonso the custodian. For now. Until... until I do not have to be Alonso the custodian any longer. I am hoping that my days of...not being Alonso *Segura* are near the end, but until this why is no more, that is all I can offer you. You deserve more, but I am asking you to hold on to your whys and hows."

I took my chance, with our closeness and his openness, to press my lips to his, hoping it was the right move.

And *oh*, it was.

We. Made. Out. In the grapes. Not far from his family's home where any of them could have seen us. Any whys and hows I had lingering could just sit back and wait their turn because this man. Was. Kissing. Me. There was groping. Heavy. Petting. And I never wanted him to stop. Though he did. And he smiled that full toothy smile again as we laughed nervously. There was that wonder...how far did we take this? Did the other person want to keep going, and where would we do that?

Now I was thinking about wheres?

"I think," he finally whispered, "that everyone will stay here tonight. Usually that is the case. There is a guesthouse where Felip and Cecilia stay when they come to visit, and there is a bedroom there for June. Tomás and Mateu still have their room, and I have the room I shared with Felip as a boy. It's not fancy..."

"Are you asking me?"

He rolled his eyes and laughed. "Would you be my guest?"

"Are you kidding me? A slice of Alonso history to explore? I would never pass that up. But...is that strange? Will your parents wonder?"

"Not when they find me on the couch in the morning."

"But until then..."

"Until then..."

He kissed me once more, took my hand and then led me back to the house. He sent me in first, and as I was passing the bathroom, I ran into Cecilia.

"Oh, Randall. I hope you don't mind, but we're all going to stay here tonight? If you have to be back in the morning, we can leave early—"

"No, no that's fine. And congratulations again. I'm excited for you."

"Thank you, and I hope you know you're coming to the

wedding. You're family to me." She smiled, and then her expression changed. "You were gone for a while. Everything okay?"

This was where I practiced being the covert operator.

"Oh, yeah. I went outside to get some air, and I talked to Felip's brother Alonso for a bit. He's really quiet, yeah?"

She wrinkled her nose. "He is. He's a great guy, very dependable, but he keeps to himself. I always feel a little bad for him, the way they all ride him. I'm looking forward to getting to know him better." She shrugged. "Okay, let's see where we can put you." She took me by the arm and led me back to the living room.

"Oh, there you are, Randall," Felip said. "Do you mind staying?"

He tried to apologize but I held up a hand. "It's fine. I didn't have anything planned for tomorrow."

He smiled. "Lo siento. I didn't even think, we usually stay. You can come with us to the guesthouse, there's a pullout couch, or—"

"He can have my room." Alonso appeared from the kitchen, toweling off his hands. "You two go ahead. I'll get him settled."

Felip gave his brother a strange look and then nodded. "Okay! Well, I'm cooking breakfast—"

"No," everyone shouted, and his mother did the sign of the cross. I couldn't help but laugh, and Felip seemed shocked.

"What? I'm a good cook."

"Sí, and you leave the biggest mess to clean up. Go to bed," his father said, shooing the happy couple off, then he pulled them back and hugged and kissed them both. "Thank you for making an old man happy."

Mrs. Segura hugged and kissed them both as well. June and Mateu parted, exchanging an odd look, and then Tomás and Mateu climbed the stairs together, pushing each other as they went.

Alonso came to my side and gestured for me to climb the stairs with him. There were more pictures of the family, some of them going back in time as we climbed and showing folks who I gathered must be grandparents, perhaps great-grandparents even. I couldn't imagine having such a long family history. I hadn't even known my grandparents, nor had I known cousins and aunts and uncles growing up. My parents had only ever seemed concerned with their immediate family unit.

At the top of the stairs, Mateu and Tomás said their good nights and headed toward the left and Alonso guided me to turn right. There was only one bedroom at this end of the second floor and there was a bathroom right outside. Alonso gestured for me to go inside, and he reached into a cabinet to fetch me a towel and a toothbrush. He didn't speak, and it was like Alonso the custodian was back.

EIGHT

SATURDAY 11:26 PM Cava Segura Winery, Pènedes, Catalonia, Spain

I took my time brushing my teeth, though I swayed on my feet. The wine had made me sleepy, and as much as I wanted to spend more time with Alonso, I worried I wouldn't be able to keep my eyes open for long.

I knocked on the bedroom door, and Alonso opened it with a faint smile, his eyes wide as if he too were unsure. He closed the door as I stood looking at the two twin beds against the wall in front of me.

"Which one was yours?" I asked him.

He gestured to the one on the left.

"Makes sense. I hadn't realized you were left-handed," I said, turning to gaze at him. "Is that a thing here? Some people get shit for being left-handed."

Alonso shook his head. "My mother is, so no. Would you like me to leave you to rest?"

"Do you *want* to leave?" I asked him, confused. I could still smell him on me from our make-out session.

"No. I don't."

"Then no. I don't want that either."

He placed his hands on my shoulders and slid my cardigan off.

"Afraid I'm going to have to retire my poor, sad sweater. I hate to. It's my favorite."

He lay it over the back of the chair at the end of the two twin beds as I kicked off my shoes. I sat on his bed and gazed up at him.

He planted his hands on his hips, that corner of his lips turned up.

I placed my hands by my sides on the bed and patted the spot next to me. That made Alonso chuckle.

"If I blow on you, you'll fall over, you're so tired."

"Don't make me sing to you."

Alonso's eyes bugged out. "¿Qué?"

I cleared my throat and let out a breathy rendition of the Aerosmith ballad. "I don't want to close my eyes. I don't want to fall asleep. I don't want to miss a thing."

The smile was back.

"That voice..." He made a clicking sound with his tongue against his teeth. He lowered himself to the bed next to me and placed his hand gently on top of mine, running his fingers over the back of my hands, in between my knuckles, which was oddly erotic to watch and to feel. I was a little mesmerized by his movements and I rested my head on his shoulder.

"I think you do need to close your eyes. Don't worry about missing anything. We may have to be patient but we will have time." He put his arm around me, kissed my temple, and then he gently pushed me over to lay my head on the pillow. "Sleep, amor." He shifted me so he could tuck me under the covers. "If I'm not here when you wake, I'll be downstairs."

"There are two beds in here," I slurred. My eyelids had grown so heavy and my breathing so deep, but before I lost all awareness, I heard Alonso whisper.

"But only one I want to be in."

I'd never been a sound sleeper, even after drinking, and I never felt comfortable sleeping at someone else's house or in hotel rooms. It had even taken me some time to get used to my new apartment.

I woke with a start and it took a minute to slow my heart rate.

Alonso sat in the rocking chair by the door, a lamp turned on above him that didn't cast much light where the beds were. His dress shirt was unbuttoned and the sleeves were rolled up. His legs were spread wide in the charcoal slacks he'd worn that evening and he had one bare foot resting on a trunk on the floor, using the leverage to gently rock the chair. He had earbuds in, and in his hands...he was working on my sweater with a needle and thread.

The man was darning the hole.

The military man, the spy, was repairing my favorite cardigan.

Be. Still. My. Heart.

I tried to be quiet, not wanting to alert him, so I could keep watching. I wondered what he was listening to. His fingers were so nimble as he handled the needle, taking care like he did with everything else, to make what I assumed would be neat stitches. He was the kind of man who had the constant shadow of a beard on his face, and it highlighted that chin dimple. I wished I'd had the opportunity to kiss him there.

He glanced up and his hands stilled as he noticed I was awake.

"You're a man of many skills, Alonso Segura." I loved saying his name. It rolled off the tongue, felt good in my mouth...

"I like to be useful." He held up the sleeve and appraised his work, then showed me that the hole had been repaired.

"Thank you. You seem to be rescuing me again, or at least my sweater."

He quirked up one side of his lips and then tied off the thread and broke it. With his teeth. Then he tapped his phone and pulled out his earbuds.

"What were you listening to?"

With a shy smile, he turned his screen around so I could see my band's second album cover on his streaming service.

"Is that weird?" he asked, and I wondered how such a man could even wonder what I'd think.

"You've most likely put your life on the line in dangerous situations, saved countless others, and yet you wonder if I think it's weird you're listening to my band? How did you even find us anyway?"

He stood from the chair, lay my sweater on the back of the chair once more, and then he walked toward the bed. He'd left the lamp on so as he walked, I had a moment to study the way he moved. His thighs were slightly bowed, his stomach flat, and he had some sort of tattoo on his chest, though I couldn't make it out. He sat hesitantly on the foot of the bed.

"I was stationed in Italy for a while and listened to a lot of their old pop music. I'd heard it growing up, Mama was a fan. It was a good way to practice my Italian. Then I was in Argentina for work back in twenty-eleven and that was when I saw Mike Patton perform the *Mondo Cane* album. It was quite an experience. I've always liked theatrical music, movie soundtracks, and of course flamenco. They help me get out of my head. Your music has that quality as well. Anyway, your album came up on my app as a recommendation and I listened. And listened. My end-of-year report even said I was in the top ten percent of your fans."

"No you were not." I ran a hand down my face and pushed up on my elbows. "It's wild to me that you would have even heard of us. I mean, outside of America. We'd played UK and Ireland before, but this last tour was our first time in the rest of Europe."

"Thank goodness for streaming services and satellite radio, then."

I wondered something. I wondered a lot of things, but I asked, "Do you play? Like your father and Felip?"

He shook his head and looked down at his hand, which he'd rested on my shin.

"No. That is their thing. I preferred to be outside as a kid. I love music, but I wanted to do my own thing. When Felip went into the service, he couldn't wait to be done so he could go off to university in America. I spent a lot of time talking to Papa about his time in the military. I liked the idea of helping people, and I was not fond of school."

I scooted over to the wall and patted the bed next to me, hoping he would join me. He did, stretching out on his back with his ankles crossed and his arms behind his head. "I was in the last group of mandatory service before the Spanish government ended the practice. Tomás and I are barely a year apart so we went together. And then I stayed on for the next twelve years. I liked it. I'm technically in what you would call the reserves, but I've been called up frequently the past few years."

"So you're...in your thirties?"

He chuckled. "Sí. Thirty-seven last month."

Ten years and a whole lifetime separated us. Would that bother him?

I turned on my side with my left arm propping my head up. I took a chance and placed my right hand on his chest, with only my fingers under the open fabric. He closed his eyes and settled into my touch.

"It's a huge sacrifice, serving in the military."

He frowned with his eyes closed. "I don't think so, not for me. It is a place to belong, someplace I can be myself but also be invisible if I want to."

"Invisible?"

"Mm. The only expectations of me are that I do my job. There's something freeing about that."

"And is that all you want?" I asked, sliding my fingers under his shirt, grazing his hardened nipple, making him hiss. His gaze shot to mine.

"Not anymore."

I tucked my hair behind my ear and I leaned down to kiss him. Immediately his hand went to my face, cradling my jaw so gently. Always with such care.

I wanted to show him the same level of care.

I pushed the sides of his shirt away. "This okay?"

"Sí."

Just as I'd hoped. I bent and planted a kiss in the middle of his chest. The tattoo was a black and gray collection of images that covered his left pec. It resembled some sort of crest, or maybe his military insignia. I'd have to ask or look it up. Later.

I couldn't believe we were here, under his sheets, in his childhood bed, with his whole family slumbering elsewhere on the grounds, and I was granted the permission to touch him. To kiss him. Actions spoke louder than words, and even though I still didn't fully understand what was happening outside of this moment, the way he'd been with his family, the way he took care of me told me all I needed to know about him.

He was a good man. And he cared for me.

It was my turn to appreciate him.

I kissed and licked his torso as he played with my hair. He remained still but for the twitches and involuntary muscle movements I took to mean he was enjoying himself. The only sound he made was his breathing, the amount of control he showed as I brought his skin to goose bumps was admirable. I'd have been moaning and thrashing, but Alonso held it in. I knew, though, that he was enjoying my touch. His lips were open, his face relaxed, and as I unfastened his slacks, his breath caught. He brought a shaky hand to help me slide them down enough to give me access.

Underneath the slacks he wore the softest black trunks. I rubbed my lips and nose over his groin, inhaling his musk, feeling the heat from his very hard cock. I nibbled over the cotton, mouthing his dick through the fabric until he swore.

"Quiero tu boca," he whispered. "Necesito tus labios, tu lengua, tus dientes. Por favor, amor."

Alonso had spoken to me more tonight than he had since I'd met him, and for once, I had no problem understanding his Spanish. Mouth, lips, tongue, and teeth. Yes, I would use them all on him. Gladly.

I got to my knees to pull his pants and trunks off all the way. I wanted him free to move. I wanted to be between his thighs. I loved giving head, always had, but Alonso himself was such a gift, and I intended to give him that care he deserved.

"You want this? Can I play?"

"Sí," he groaned softly.

I knelt before him on the bed and ran my hands over the curves of his inner thighs, stroking him below his sac with my thumbs. All that skin, the color of smoky quartz and covered with dark hair, soft on his torso and arms, and coarse and curly everywhere else, was a delight to all of my senses. He was solid, his muscles thick, but not cut like a bodybuilder. I wanted to keep touching, but my mouth was…hungry for him.

"Roll on your side?" I asked as I lay beside him and scooted down. I wrapped my arm around his hips, holding his lower half tight against my chest, and continued savoring him, nestling my cheek against his hipbone, kissing everywhere I could until his legs were trembling so much that I knew he needed me.

And I loved being needed.

I looked up into his eyes and he ran a hand over the top of my head.

"Tan bonic."

I felt beautiful. I felt…seen. That was what was so wonderful about Alonso. He *saw* me, never asked for anything or wanted me for anything other than…me. What a stellar gift he was.

I took him into my mouth and retained eye contact with him as he began to slowly, shakily move his hips, thrusting in and out of my ecstatic mouth, all while continuing to gaze at me in wonder and stroke my hair. I gripped his ass, loving the feel of his muscles flexing, twitching as he moved, and I let my fingers graze between them, keeping my gaze on his, hoping he was—

He let out a long, quiet moan as I touched his hole, and his hips bucked, his rhythm gone. I didn't know if he had any lube, and I didn't want to hurt him, but apparently the light pressure was enough for him, because he grabbed my jaw and his back arched.

"Randall, I—"

I nodded, still looking up at him, and I pulled off, leaving my tongue on the underside of his cock as he came with a harsh gasp. He filled my mouth with his spend and I continued to lick him until he shuddered and placed a firm hand on my shoulder.

He never stopped watching me.

"Fes-me un petó. Un beso, por favor. Si us plau."

I frowned, and he pulled me up face-to-face with him and chuckled. He was panting and his chest was damp with perspiration.

"Kiss me," he said, and I so did. He whimpered as he tasted himself on my tongue and it made me ridiculously happy that he seemed so pleased.

"You bounce back and forth between Spanish and Catalan and I'm still trying to learn the first one," I said when he paused to breathe.

He smiled and pressed his forehead to mine. "You need to learn both. Keep up, amor."

Amor. He'd said that before. Why did I think he really meant it, that I was his love?

All I could do was smile back at him.

Once his breathing slowed he looked me up and down. "You seem to be overdressed."

My cheeks burned. How did I tell him that I was much more comfortable with *him* naked than me? "Oh." I started to get up. "Let me just turn off the lights."

"Randall, wait." Alonso sat up. "Is everything all right?"

"Yeah," I said, my voice cracking. I turned off the light, then I unbuttoned my dress shirt and took it off in the dark, laying it with my sweater. At least I thought I had. I took off my pants and set them on the chair too and went back to the bed in my t-shirt and boxers. I climbed back into the bed against the wall and under the covers. "Sorry, I take up a lot of space."

Alonso stopped my squirming movements with a hand to my cheek.

"Stop," he said quietly. "You're good. You're more than good. I like you very much. All of you." He ran a hand down my chest, over my t-shirt. "I want you to be comfortable, but I want to touch you. Are you hiding from me?"

"I'm not hiding," I said with a sigh. I didn't want to make a big deal of our physical differences. It was my own issue to contend with. He hadn't seemed to be bothered by the extra me, so I shouldn't be either.

"Good," he said, grabbing my ass and pulling my front flush to his. "Because if you want to spend the night in my childhood bed with me, we should really act out all of my teenaged fantasies."

I burst out laughing but his hand caught most of the sound. We pressed our foreheads together and continued to snicker, pulling the covers over our heads.

"Be quiet," I said. "Your parents are going to hear." But I couldn't stop smiling.

"You are the one who needs to be quiet. I can't wait to reciprocate."

And he did, sucking me off reverently, just as I had him, and once more we watched each other. It was darker now, but I could still make out his eyes in the pale light from the window. I couldn't believe that this incredible man, who knew who I was, who saw me for all that I was, would so enthusiastically go down on me. He was quiet, yes, but his grip was firm, even when I tried to pull away. He ran one hand up over my belly and for once it didn't take me out of the moment. With the other hand he held on tight to my ass, encouraging me to move, to thrust as he had. My skin prickled with sweat, and with a zing up my spine, I knew I was close.

"Alonso?" I whispered, and he nodded. He groaned around me, pulled me tighter to him, taking me deeper, and when I came, I bit my fist to keep from singing his praises.

He was kissing me a moment later, his tongue salty, his stubble wet, and he was noisy as he sucked and licked at my lips. Perhaps I'd discovered just what it took for him to lose control. The victory eased my worries that I somehow wouldn't be enough—or would be too much—for him. He desired me, and that was what I should take from this encounter, especially since it might be some time until we could be together like this again.

I didn't want to waste a moment.

He paused his kisses to catch his breath and he asked me if I needed anything.

"For this night to not end?"

He smiled sadly and ran a thumb over my lip. "I wish this as well. Let me hold you until the last possible second, when I must retire to the couch downstairs and pretend as if I had not been ravaged all night."

"So I probably shouldn't give you a big hickey," I joked, and his eyes flared.

"Not where someone might see."

I left a few marks on him, and him on me. We explored each other as much as two grown men—both pushing two hundred pounds—could in a twin bed in a house filled with people sleeping soundly.

Alonso's phone alarm chirped at five AM when we were both on the verge of a second coming.

"You must come before the other cock crows," he whispered, and I laughed, losing our rhythm, but I managed to keep hold of his cock, allowing him to reach his climax. His whole body shook and he gasped as his warmth filled my hand. I smiled a satisfied smile.

"I'm sorry," he said, kissing me one last time. "I hate to leave you."

"It's okay," I said, enjoying the show as he got dressed and I saw the love bites on his ass. When we returned to work Monday, I'd know they were there under his coveralls. It would help. A little. Maybe not. "I hope you get some rest today. I'm not sorry I kept you up."

He bent over the bed one last time. "I'm only sorry I have to leave you."

And that was it, wasn't it? He had to leave, would have to keep his distance, for who knew how long.

My smile faltered, but then I took a Randall 2.0 breath. "I'm glad we had tonight."

"We'll have many more," he said, kissing me once last time. When he reached the door, he turned to face me. "Count on that, Randall Sutter. I'm coming for you when this is over."

I grinned and snuggled into the pillow we'd shared. "I can't wait."

It stung a bit, though, eating breakfast later that morning, watching Felip and Cecilia chatting happily about wedding plans with Mr. and Mrs. Segura, and Tomás and Mateu carrying on a lively conversation about going to see FC Barcelona play later in the week. All we could do was nudge each other's toes under the table a few times and sneak adoring glances.

"Felip, you should come with us before you go back to California," Tomás said, interrupting him.

"Ah, I don't know...Cecilia—"

"Wants you to get your fútbol fix in before you go back to California and complain about American football."

He took her hand and kissed it. "Can I convince you to come with us?"

The brothers pleaded with her and she rolled her eyes.

"Only if Randall comes with me," she said, dragging me into the deal.

"Excellent. Mateu, you can get us the box?"

"Sí, sí. Alonso, you coming?"

Alonso had been clearing the table around us and he turned to look at his brothers. "If I am able."

Their enthusiasm waned a little but they continued to talk about the game, and Cecilia gave me a grateful look.

She signed thank you.

No problem. As long as it doesn't interfere with work.

She nodded and pursed her lips.

Felip gave her a look and sighed. "I swear I'll watch all the, how do you call them, Gold Miners—"

"Oh my God," she said. "Like you didn't live in the Bay Area while you were in college. You know exactly who the Forty-Niners are, and yes, you *will* watch with me."

Of course he would. He would do anything for her, and I was grateful. I was happy to see her happy.

I was happy this morning. And judging by the handful of looks I caught from Alonso, he was as well.

NINE

MONDAY, Noon, Frederick Douglass International School, Castelldefels, Catalonia, Spain

"Tell us everything." Josette, Camille, and Sasha sat with me for lunch on Monday and were itching for details of my adventure at the winery.

"And I mean *everything* because when we came to get you for brunch on Sunday, you were not home." Josette tapped a finger against her lip.

"You're a good detective," was all I'd say. I continued eating my bocadillo and tried hard to minimize the smug grin on my face.

Sasha leaned in close. "Does that mean you had a *salaciously* good time?"

"Since you three obviously won't let it go," I said dramatically, though in reality I wanted very much to tell them everything. I was bursting at the seams to talk about my weekend. This would be a true test of my clandestine skills. "The whole story is that we went to Cava Segura, we had a delicious meal, my friend Cecilia and her fiancé Felip Segura announced they'd be having their wedding at the winery in June, we drank a lot of really good wine, and we all stayed overnight in the Seguras' home. They fixed a lovely brunch on Sunday, I got home around three in the afternoon, and went straight to bed until this morning when my alarm didn't go off and I had to rush to work. Satisfied?"

"That's wonderful! Can you get us an invite to a tasting up there?" Camille asked. "I've not been to one of the fancy Spanish wineries. Do not tell my parents but I much prefer cava to champagne."

"You are disowned as a French girl," Sasha said, and they giggled together.

"I would have to ask Cecilia if they're open to the public. I think they are?"

Then they asked about the food, they asked about Cecilia and Felip and how they met. And then Alonso passed through the cafeteria and I lost track of what I was saying.

"Perhaps you had too much fun," Camille said, chuckling as I frowned and tried to gather my thoughts. Thoughts other than he's got my love bites under those coveralls. He kept his gaze straightforward, but he did look toward our table once and I thought his lip twitched, but I could have been imagining it.

I was completely obliterated when it came to him. I would follow protocol, only greet him as a colleague, and I would definitely not swoon. That would be difficult, but I couldn't act familiar with him at all. We'd discussed the ground rules before we parted Sunday morning.

"If I do not look your way in the hall, know that I'll be missing you terribly." He'd caught me in the hallway outside the bathroom before we'd left the Segura house, while Tomás and Mateu had Felip occupied and Cecilia was saying goodbye to his parents outside. "I hope this is all over soon. I want to bring you back here as mine."

"You mean, just spring me on your family, like, 'surprise!'?"

He'd grinned and gripped my hip. I would miss his hands.

"Why not? I hope we can come to Felip's wedding together. I want to dance with you."

"That would be wonderful, and a long time from now."

"I know," he'd said. "I wish I could tell you—"

"I know. Until then, I will do my best to pretend I'm not thinking about you every other second..."

His expression went solemn and he took my hand in both of his. "Be patient. I have a feeling that things are going to develop swiftly in the coming days. Be careful, and be patient with me, por favor, amor."

"Amor. Is that Spanish or Catalan?"

He leaned in to kiss my cheek. "Both. Start practicing in earnest. You need to keep up."

As he'd walked away, a shiver had run through me. I'd be patient. I hoped *he* would be careful. Whatever this mission? Case? Situation? Whatever he was involved in, I had to imagine that as a member of military intelligence—okay I'd started to do a search online but then paranoia set in. If he was at Frederick Douglass, that had to mean there was a counterpoint to his work, and that could mean I was being watched, any of us were being monitored. For all I knew, there were bugs in my apartment...

Wow, I'd watched one too many James Bond films. Or maybe episodes of *Chuck*. Oh, God. Was I Chuck Bartowski in this scenario? The hapless everyman who stumbled across something I shouldn't have? I had no idea. All I knew was that I'd met a nearly perfect man who actually wanted to spend time with me, and that I was falling hard for him.

"Too much fun indeed," Sasha said, waving a hand in front of my face.

"Oh, uh, yeah. It was fun. I need to get ready for my next class." I stood, bussed my tray, and hurried to my classroom as they laughed at me. Thankfully Monday was all private lessons, because I was so distracted, I was liable to flub up with my students.

When I opened the door with my key, a one-word note slipped out of the doorjamb.

Soon.

I heard the wheels of Alonso's cart and turned around in time to catch him smile at me and then continue on his way.

Ah. So he was going to be cute about it.

I smiled the rest of the afternoon.

The next day when I returned from lunch with the French Foreign Legion, as I'd started to call them, I discovered a book of poetry in Catalan on my desk. No note, just the book.

I got the hint.

On Thursday I went to the office during lunch for a check-in meeting with Lara.

"Everything is going okay?"

"More than, thank you. I'm so happy this job found me."

She laughed. "I've had nothing but praise from the parents. I only wish we'd had you long enough to prepare something for Three Kings Day. Are you aware of how they celebrate Christmas differently in Spain, and specifically in Catalonia?"

"I'm not, but I'll look it up."

"It's too soon, but perhaps you could put together some sort of short program, a winter concert? End of January?"

"I can definitely do that," I said to her. I was already mentally cataloguing which kids were close to ready and which pieces could be ready with a bit more work.

Lara beamed. "I'm so glad you are here. See you at Friday Social?"

"Yes, ma'am."

She waved as I left her office. When I reached my room, I paused because the door was open. I always locked my door. Perhaps Alonso was inside? I opened the door and there was a daisy laying on the shelf inside the door, which wasn't there before. It looked like one of the yellow daisies off the bushes outside the school. I was feeling all kinds of *awww* about it... until I noticed another surprise.

On a table at the back of the room was a guitar case, the size and shape of an acoustic guitar.

My heart fluttered and my cheeks warmed. What a sweet gesture.

Then it hit me.

Would Alonso have taken such a chance? He could have hidden a flower, but anyone might have seen him go into my room with a guitar. Should I touch it? Should I—

My next student arrived, and I had no more time to investigate. For the next three hours, I entertained child after child with stories of my early years as a musician and asked them to tell me what they loved and loathed about playing. I didn't want music lessons to be something they hated. So many kids were turned off by them in their early years, so I made it a point to give kids several entry points to falling in love with the art.

At the end of the day, I was still wondering about the guitar when I heard the wheels of Alonso's cart outside. Would he come in, or was he going to avoid me at every opportunity?

He came in and paused when he saw me.

"Hi."

Totally normal way to greet the custodian at my workplace that I definitely only had contact with at work.

He nodded, glanced behind him to see if anyone was in the hall, and he pulled the door semi closed.

"¿Y eso?

"Huh? Um..." I pointed to the flower, which I'd put in a cup with water. His cheeks flushed.

"No sé, señor." He gave a sly grin, but then he caught sight of the guitar, and he frowned.

"Was this you, too?" I asked in a whispered voice.

He shook his head and pulled the door the rest of the way shut. Then he hurried over to the phone and dialed the office. He said something in Catalan and hung up.

"What should I do?"

He put a finger to his lips and shook his head. "No toques la guitarra," he whispered before leaving the room.

My heart was pounding. I knew it was too easy to think the guitar was from Alonso. Then who? Someone had been in my room, and that made me nervous. With all of the eyes on campus, who could have snuck in and done this?

Parents were filing in and lining up outside of the classrooms to pick up their children. The main building, where my music room was located, had classrooms on each side of a large atrium so there was plenty of room for parents to wait. Many of them came early or stayed late after drop-off and sat around chatting. I thought it was kind of cool that they had a place for community as well.

I heard raised voices out in the hallway so I turned for the door.

Mr. Ferrer, the man he'd been with in the parking lot that day, and the two bodyguard looking types with them had cornered a couple and were shouting at them in Catalan.

Lara went running over and I followed, just so she had a little backup. Not that I could do much, but I wasn't a small guy.

"What is going on here?" She stared down Ferrer with her hands on her hips.

I caught Alonso's movement out of the corner of my eye. He stepped out from behind a pillar and circled around behind Ferrer and Vidal.

"Perdó, senyora Trujillo-Perez, but this is none of your concern." Ferrer turned that smile on her that made my stomach turn. Instead of seeming annoying and arrogant like he had in my classroom, though, today his look felt menacing.

"It is my concern if it is happening in my school. Now, please. Return to your vehicles and I will escort your children out."

Ferrer looked as if he would argue, but then he followed her direction. Vidal, however stood his ground. He spoke to the couple again in Catalan, but one phrase I caught—brigada de neteja, or cleaning brigade, which was what they called the people who went around and removed the independence flags and propaganda from the town—I recalled hearing at the Seguras on Saturday, when they were talking about the conflict between the independistas and those wishing to remain a part of Spain.

So the conflict in Catalonia had surfaced in our little school. A few of the other adults stood around watching the goings-on carefully. I wondered how many people here were on each side? Was it like being a Democrat at the Republican National Convention? Or like a Hillary supporter at a MAGA rally? Neither would be comfortable, but would one be more liable to erupt into violence?

A police car pulled into the parking lot and parked outside of the doors. Two officers got out and stood near their car as the bell rang to release the students.

Within a few moments, everyone seemed to scatter. I looked to see where Ferrer went, worried about Pere. I hated that his father was making such a fuss at school. How would this impact Pere's relationships with his peers?

I stuck around out in the hall, as did the other staff, until all of the children and adults were out of the building. Lara then addressed us as a group.

"Thank you all for being so vigilant. Keep your eyes open and call me at any time if you are concerned. I spoke to the police and they will be here in the mornings and afternoons until things have settled down."

She thanked us again and the rest of the staff began returning to their rooms to pack up and go home.

I looked for Alonso. He was having a conversation with the couple who'd been harassed. The man was gesturing wildly with his hands and the woman wiped at her eyes, but she was frowning and spoke in clipped words.

The situation had been volatile. We couldn't have this happening at our school. I was beginning to think this was why Alonso was here. What might these people have to do with the larger political movement? Were they actually dangerous, the parents of my students? Alonso had said he thought things might ramp up soon. Did that mean he had information? Had he known this would happen today? I was going to make myself nuts with my questions.

I stopped by the office but Lara's office was closed and Madame Lahlou said she was not to be disturbed. Had Alonso told them about the guitar? He'd called the office from my classroom. *Man, I really need to learn Catalan. Or Spanish.* What should I do?

There was nothing I *could* do but lock up my classroom and call it a day.

I made my way home still thinking about the separatists. I

paid closer attention to my environment and noticed that yes, there were several houses and apartments that had the Catalan flag hanging from their balconies. Mr. Segura had said that outside Barcelona proper, there were more folks who felt strongly that Catalonia should secede. What a strange time to be living in this place. Would things erupt? Could there be a civil war again? Was it safe?

Honestly, living in the United States could be dangerous at any time, especially in the last few years. Therefore, while this situation was tense, how was it different than the US? Depending on which news program you watched, we were days away from a breakdown in our democracy.

Schools were no longer the safe places in North America that my parents and grandparents experienced, either. During my student teaching, we'd had to lock down the school because a student was rumored to have a weapon. Turned out he did, but he hadn't taken it out of his bag. He'd also had written a suicide note. I knew anything was possible in a school. I guess I had a false sense of security here in Spain because they didn't seem to have as many issues with guns. But guns weren't the only things to fear.

Friday afternoon, Pere Ferrer's father was late again, so we kept going with the lesson. Forty-five minutes after the end of school, Alonso came by with his cart and peeked his head in. I'd been hoping to see him all day to ask about the guitar, which remained on the back table untouched. I waved to him that it was okay for him to come in, but he held up a hand and continued on his way. I sat beside Pere and he played what he'd learned of the song he wanted to play for his father.

"Wonderful, Pere. I'm so proud of you."

"What wonderful thing has my son done?"

Pere and I both turned to look at his father standing in the doorway.

"Papa! I have a surprise for you for next week's party!"

Pere ran to his father and he gave him a big hug. The kid came up to his father's belly button and his father, for once, actually hugged him like he was happy to see him.

Then he turned his attention to me. "Pere, why don't you meet me at the car?" He pulled out his ID, held it up in his hand with a wink, and scanned it without prompt from me. Pere grabbed his bag and waved to me as he darted out the door.

"Pere is doing great on piano. He's a natural."

"Mm, so I hear. According to my wife, he's been practicing at home with his keyboard and headphones for hours. Do you know what his surprise is?"

I stood from the piano bench and shoved my hands in my pockets. It had been such a weird week. I didn't think my adrenaline had slowed at all, and I needed to be so cautious around this man, it took all of my remaining energy to keep focused around him.

"I'm not at liberty to discuss," I said, pretending to lock my lips with a key. Professional, a little humorous, but that was a far as I would go.

"That is all right. I shall find out next week. Speaking of which, I hope you received my invitation?" He gestured to the table with the guitar.

I'd been trying to ignore it all day. Lara told me at lunch that she and Alonso had talked and discovered that it had been delivered to the school and left in the office. Madame Lahlou apparently had placed it in my room and forgotten to let the others know.

"Invitation?"

He smiled and walked closer to the guitar. He reached under the case and pulled out an envelope. I hadn't even noticed. Had Alonso? "Ah, here it is. Sí. I am having a gathering at my house, and I would love for you to make an appearance. Play some songs, talk to some of the guests. I understood you lost your guitar in a robbery in Barcelona, so I thought I would offer you one of mine."

The air huffed out of my lungs. "I can't...I can't accept that. I appreciate it."

He opened the case, picked up the guitar, and then he strummed it, making sure it was tuned properly. It had such a warm, beautiful tone. My fingers twitched.

"It is one of many I have played. I want you to have it. My son talks about you nonstop." At this, his smile turned sour. "Of course, children like what is cool and hip, isn't that right?"

"Mr. Ferrer, I appreciate the offer and the invitation—"

"Senyor Sutter, is this what you want? To be a music teacher?"

"I—I love teaching. I love the kids."

"But you wish to be onstage, do you not? You may be a quiet, unassuming man in person, but I've seen video of your performance. You're very compelling to watch." He moved closer to me and sweat broke out along my back, but this wasn't nerves I was feeling.

It was fear.

"I might be able to help you get back to what you were doing before this...detour." He looked around the room as he stopped about a foot and a half from me. "I know people in the industry, Randall." He smiled and placed a hand on my shoulder. My stomach roiled at the gesture.

I cleared my throat and stepped back enough to force him to let go. "I'm afraid it would seem...improper. I'm not supposed to spend time with families outside of school—"

He chuckled. "You are worried about senyora Trujillo-

Perez? Fear not. I have many friends on the board of directors for the school. She will bend to my will."

He said it so matter-of-factly that my blood ran cold. Did he actually have this much power or was he full of shit?

I kicked up my chin. "Regardless, I'll have to run anything I do that's school-adjacent by her. You understand, I'm sure. I don't want to lose my job and have to leave the country." I smiled confidently and it was enough to get him to back up a bit.

He nodded finally and smiled. "Very well. Think on it. The gathering is next Saturday in the evening. All of the details are in the invitation. There will be representatives of the music industry in Spain there, as well as members of our school community, of course. It is a formal event. You may bring a guest. I would love to have you play for us, but if this is too much for you, I understand. You are in a foreign country. I would hate for you to be in a precarious situation."

Something told me that was exactly what he wanted. He was definitely a man who liked to use his position to intimidate people. He was also a man who was so hot and cold with his own kid that I didn't feel I could respect him.

"I appreciate your understanding."

He backed up toward the door and then gestured once more to the guitar. "Consider it a loan, then. A guitarist cannot be without his instrument, yes?" He pointed to the envelope he'd left on the table next to the guitar case. "Be sure to RSVP. Have a nice weekend, senyor Sutter."

"You, too."

Ferrer strolled out the door, tapping it twice on his way out.

And then I breathed.

Holy shit.

I was still standing there, bent over with my hands on my thighs a few moments later, when Alonso came in and shut the door behind him. He walked straight to me and held my face in his hands.

"Are you alright, amor?" he whispered.

I blinked and pulled his hands away. "Alonso, I don't—"

The door opened and Lara breezed in, shutting the door behind her.

I stepped away from Alonso.

"It's all right, Randall," Lara said, placing a hand on my arm.

Alonso pulled out a mechanical device and walked toward the guitar.

"What are you—"

Lara held her finger up to her lips.

We watched as Alonso held the device over the guitar, then he shook his head. He continued around the room with it, and Lara took me by the arms.

"Randall, I need to talk to you about something serious, okay? And I'm sorry to bring you into this, but we need your help."

I frowned and looked to Alonso's back as he finished his sweep of the room.

"It's clear. I checked yesterday before I left. Nothing showed up except mine and nothing new has been placed in here since I checked yesterday."

His what?

"Randall, this is Sargento Alonso Segura with Ejercito de Tierra, the Spanish Army, and he's here investigating some disturbing activity. As I'm sure you're aware, there have been some incidents on campus lately involving some of the parents."

I couldn't stop staring at Alonso.

"We had a feeling Mr. Ferrer is involved, so we've been monitoring him along with several other parents."

Alonso still hadn't spoken, and he had to know what I was thinking.

As if I'd communicated telepathically, he cleared his throat. "What did he say to you?" he asked.

"He, uh, had the guitar delivered to the school and someone in the office put it in here during lunch." After getting robbed, this felt like a violation. I knew it was a classroom and not the same as private property, but I didn't like the idea that anyone could come in here. We had valuable instruments and equipment. What if I'd had personal items stored inside?

Lara frowned and looked to Alonso. "No one should be coming into classrooms other than you, me, or teachers. I'll let the office staff know to be more careful and we'll let you know if anything else is delivered."

"What did he say just now?" Alonso repeated.

"He asked me to come to a gathering next weekend at his home. I think he wants me to play? I don't know. He mentioned some music industry people... Look, Lara, I'm not going to go. I know the rules—"

"Actually, maybe you should go." Lara looked between us, and my heart pounded out of control. What could she possibly mean? That would be breaking all of the rules.

"But I want to stay here. I love my job."

"What? Of course you do, Randall. This isn't...no, you're not in any trouble here." She gave me a quick hug. I probably looked as distraught as I felt.

"I will discuss with my commander and we will determine what is best. I am not willing to put Randall...er, señor Sutter, in any danger."

So what was the scowl about then? Was he angry with me? Angry at Lara or Ferrer? Had I overstepped?

"If he goes to the gathering, perhaps he may hear something?"

Alonso's scowl deepened.

"Did he say anything else?"

I shook my head. "No. I was kind of in shock about the guitar. I can't believe he brought it. He said he knew what happened, about us getting robbed in Barcelona? How would he know that?"

"It's probably been on the news, and on social media." Lara shrugged. "Maybe he heard it from someone? Did you tell your students?"

"No," I said, trying to think. "No, not even the older kids. All I've said is that I was in an American indie rock band for a while before I decided to take this job. I haven't even told them the name of the band, although I guess they could have Googled me. But would they?"

Lara smiled. "I'm sure they did. All kids are nosy and curious. Okay, let's wait for Alonso to speak to his commander to decide what to do. I want you to be confident, Randall, that whatever you are asked to do, it is your decision, and that none of this will negatively impact your job. You seem to have gained the Ferrers' trust and might be in a unique position to help us. We've had some complaints in our community of powerful people using intimidation to try to sway public favor about the separatist movement. Some of our parents are feeling unsafe with their children here, and I don't want to lose students because of this, nor do I want anyone to be put in danger."

I looked to Alonso, who had gone quiet, and wondered if I would get a chance to speak to him.

"Well, we won't keep you," Lara said, seeming to catch on to the tension between us. "I'd still love to see you tonight at Friday Social. I think we could all use a drink after this week. Alonso, why don't you join us? Maybe some of the other teachers will have some news to share?"

He nodded. "Sí. I will come. I want to be sure Randall gets home safely."

I hoped my relief wasn't too obvious. I desperately needed to ask all the whats: what the fuck was going on? What the hell did he expect me to do? And what about poor Pere? One what seemed obvious, though. This issue of separatists was apparently the why he was there, the why behind his actions, avoiding me, etc.

"Excellent. Pack up. Let's get out of here for a much-needed weekend."

Lara turned and left the room, leaving me alone with Alonso.

"Amor, I don't like this," he whispered. Apparently he had a monitoring device in my classroom and perhaps others were listening. "Let's go," he said a little louder.

"What about that?" I asked him, pointing to the guitar.

He shook his head and gestured for me to leave it.

I grabbed my messenger bag and slipped my laptop in it before pulling the strap over my head. Alonso reached over and tugged my hair out from under the strap.

"¿Estás listo?"

I nodded and walked out the door ahead of him, his hand on my lower back grounding me so I didn't lose my shit.

We got out to the parking lot and I stopped near the bike rack.

"Why don't you leave it? I will drive you."

"You mean you get to be seen with me now?"

His lip turned up. "Get in the car."

He led me to an ancient-looking Saab convertible and unlocked my door with the key, holding it open. I thanked him and climbed in. The car was spotless inside, but there were small cracks in the dash and the leather. It smelled really good inside. Like Alonso's cologne, which was subtle but made my mouth water.

He climbed in and shut the door, taking a deep breath before he looked at me.

"This is what you meant by things happening soon?"

"Sí, pero I didn't want for you to be involved."

"But now that I am?"

He slid his hand over my thigh and squeezed gently. "I will keep you safe. I won't leave your side."

I put my hand over his. "Like at all?"

He linked our hands together. "You wouldn't mind?"

"Not. At. All."

He shook his head, but he smiled. "I would like that too. What I don't like is involving you in this situation, Randall. The reason I'm here...it's not good. If I'm involved, it's never good."

"So we work together. To make it better." I bumped him with my shoulder. "You know, he told me to bring a guest to his house..."

"I don't want you in his house." His firm voice would have terrified me if I didn't recognize the protectiveness in it.

"But if it helps? I want to help. If it keeps the kids safe—"

"I want *you* safe, amor. This is not your fight. These people are not... This is more than the movement. It's more than that going on." He cursed, turning toward the window and rubbing at his lips.

"These people are our school community, and if the kids are at risk, then I want to help. And if I stay..." Which I wanted more than anything. I loved my new community. My school, my French Foreign Legion...Alonso. His family. They were so fun and welcoming to me, although I wished they would give their son a break. If they had any idea what he was doing, I hoped they would treat him better. "If I stay here in Castelldefels, or in Barcelona, then it affects me too, right?"

"Do you know what this means? Going in with a listening device or a wire? And then if the families find out you are involved, that could make it impossible for you to keep working here, and that is not what you want. I know."

I took a deep breath and turned in my seat to face him. "I am worried about Pere. Whatever his father is or isn't doing, it's impacting him. You should see him, he's working so hard to impress his father, and Ferrer treats him like an afterthought. I know how that feels."

Alonso met my gaze. "Your family does not support you?"

I shrugged with one shoulder. "They don't know I'm here. They haven't called or checked in since before we came to Europe in early summer. I should reach out. I kind of fucked things up with my father last year and, well, I suppose I should get over myself and call them, but I spent so many years being told to get a real job, to stop chasing a fantasy. Now that I've failed, I kinda don't want to hear it."

Saying it out loud was like a blow to the chest. My eyes filled with tears and it took a minute for my chin to stop quivering.

"You failed nothing. You had a real job, you *have* a real job now. To make music is not a fantasy. You are good at it. You make people happy with your music. You just didn't have the right job for your family, and that is *their* problem."

He brushed my hair back from my face and turned my chin to face him.

"It's not *your* problem."

I tried on a smile. "You sound like you know a little about that. Your family seemed to give you a hard time." I hoped I wasn't out of line bringing it up, but if we were in this together, I wanted him to know that I saw him, too.

"You picked up on that, eh?" He looked away and let his

hand fall back to my thigh. "I might know something about having the wrong job for my family."

I wiped at my eye. "So, does that mean we are two wrongs who, together, make a right?"

That got me a shy smile. He glanced around to see that we were alone in the parking lot, sitting in his car in a dark corner. "I like that. Come here."

I felt his kiss down to my toes, which curled inside my canvas shoes. Every breath, every moan echoed in the small car. His scent filled my sinuses, his grip was firm on my face, on my thigh. A few more moments and the windows would fog up, and I'd abandon all propriety. I was ready to climb over the console when his movements slowed, his tongue gave one last brush against mine. It was over quickly, but I'd remember this one. This kiss was like signing a contract, making a pact. Alonso and me against the world. Or, at least against the current threat to our community.

"Let me take you to the social before I molest you any further." He started the car while I laughed, and he squealed his tires pulling out of the parking lot.

It would have been a quick drive to this week's bar in the city center but the road was blocked for some reason we couldn't see.

"May I?" I asked, reaching for the knob on the radio.

He chuckled. "You may, but the antenna is broken and I only have cassettes. They're in the glove box."

"Ooo, so this car is a classic in more ways than one. What year is this?"

"It was my uncle's. He bought it in nineteen ninety-six? Felip and our cousin Jose turned it down when he was ready to give it up, but I didn't need anything fancy. And I love putting the top down."

I used the flashlight on my phone to look at the tapes he had.

"Holy shit, Jeff Buckley? My idol. *Grace* was the first album I bought when I started my vinyl collection. We have a great record store in Grass Valley. Clocktower Records. As soon as I had enough money from my first job, I bought a portable turntable, you know the kind in the suitcase? And I bought *Grace*."

I popped in the cassette and it started at the beginning of "Lover You Should Have Come Over." I couldn't help myself. I started to sway and then I was singing, and it came straight from the heart. What was this life, driving through Castelldefels with the most wonderful man, in the funkiest old car, with my favorite singer coming through a decent set of speakers? I wondered if we'd ever get to drive along the beach with the top down, my hair blowing in my face as I sang at the top of my lungs. At this very moment, I wanted that more than anything.

We finally got to the problem in the road and reality was there to suck the wind out of my daydreaming.

"A protest," I said as I turned off the music. "Is it—"

"Anti-independencia. And pro-independence on the other side of the road." He followed the directions of the traffic cop, which took us around several blocks before we could get anywhere near the bar. Once Alonso found a spot to park, he turned off the engine.

"I want you to go inside," he said quietly. "I need to call my commanding officer. If I can come in, I will. If he says for me to keep my distance, I will text you and I will wait outside for you. I want to take you home."

His words, while spoken seriously, gave me a thrill. He probably meant he would take me home as a precaution, but I wanted him to *come home* with me.

"All right. But when you come in...am I supposed to, like, *know you* know you?"

Alonso scrubbed at his stubble and I saw the cracks...he was tired. Did he sleep? When he was on an assignment such as this, did he get down time? I knew he'd had some sleep Saturday night, but that was not enough. And where was he staying?

"Keep your phone handy. I will text you."

"Okay. With instructions?"

He nodded. A smile teased the corners of his lips but then he took my hands. "Randall, no matter what my commander says, whatever my cover is to be, I need you to know...how we are, how we have been when we are alone, this is real for me. It's not work. I don't go undercover often, and after this assignment...I'm not likely to volunteer for anything like this again. It's been too close. I don't like pretending. I'm not an actor. I do my job, and sometimes that means doing things I don't like or don't want to do, things that aren't me." He exhaled and frowned. "I don't know how to say this other than I don't want you to think that I am not being true with you."

And the thrill was back.

"Oh, baby. I appreciate that very much. I'll trust you."

"Please," he said, his voice breathy. "Because I don't know what will happen."

I pressed my palm to his cheek. "It'll be okay," I said, though I didn't know if I should be trying to reassure him. "I'll go inside and let you do what you need to." I ran my thumb over his lip and blew out a breath. I could do this. I could be brave for Alonso.

Or maybe I'd only been acting brave, and really this would prove to be too much.

TEN

FRIDAY 5:46 PM City Center, Castelldefels, Catalonia, Spain

The group was all gathered at a high-top table and had already had a few drinks, judging by the noise level. I made my way straight to Lara and gave her a hug.

"Where's Alonso?" she asked in my ear.

"In the car. Making a call." I kissed her on the cheek before stepping away.

"You okay?" she asked me, wrinkling her nose.

Are you kidding? "I'm great. You need a refill?" She said no as Camille called me over to the French Foreign Legion's end of the table.

"We got your Segura for you," she said, and I tripped over a jacket on the floor. *My Segura.* I liked the sound of that.

I gave them each kisses and took a chair on the end next to Camille. I was getting natural finally with this whole cheek-kissing greeting business.

"I worried you weren't coming," Josette said, leaning close to talk over the noise. "Are you okay? I heard about the scene in the atrium. Can you believe it?"

My pocket buzzed and I pulled out my phone.

I'm coming in. Play along.

I had no idea what that meant.

I tried not to look around and instead attempted to follow the conversation. I was listening to Ivan ask Sasha about where he should visit in the South of France, and since the three women had attended university in Montpellier, they were telling him the good things to see there. I caught sight of Alonso entering the bar. I knew I was supposed to act casual, like I didn't *know him* know him, but I had butterflies in my belly watching him make his way through the tables over to where we were sitting. He'd said to play it cool, but sitting here keeping a great big secret from everyone was, well, making me hella nervous.

"Alonso. Bona nit," Lara said, and he walked directly toward her, not glancing in my direction. He kissed her cheek, and she waved for the table to pay attention. He was good at this whole undercover gig. Way better than me.

"Everyone, I'm not sure if you've all had a chance to meet Alonso. He was so kind as to step in for Pedro when he hurt his back and he's doing a wonderful job of taking care of our students." She repeated herself in Spanish and everyone waved and said hello.

"Mucho gusto," he said with a shy wave, and then he looked around the table for a place to sit.

"Down here...aquí," Josette said, waving her hands and pointing to an empty chair she'd pulled between us. She leaned in close to Sasha and Camille and spoke in French.

"No fair," I whispered. "I can't understand any of you."

Camille spoke next to my ear. "We have a bet going on to see who he prefers."

My eyes bugged out. "What do you mean?"

Sasha leaned in close. "He's so handsome, but no one knows anything about him. We'll sit him next to you and see who he pays more attention to."

I rolled my eyes. "Oh my God, it doesn't work like that. Not all the gays are attracted to each other." They were ridiculous.

"No, but you are so pretty, and men can't resist Camille, so we will see what happens."

Is it fair to take their money? "Leave me out of it," I said as Alonso took his seat. *I wonder if my love bite is still visible. The one he's sitting on right now.*

The bar erupted in applause and music as karaoke started up. We were usually gone before they started the music, but folks seemed to want to be together tonight. I wondered if they'd been as shaken as I was by today's unrest.

Camille leaned across me and spoke in perfect, I assumed, Catalan to him. His eyes brightened and he replied to her. *God, he's hot.* If I didn't know he was bisexual, I'd think he was totally into Camille by the way he was speaking to her.

"Oh, Camille," Sasha said, elbowing her friend. "I didn't know you spoke Catalan so well. How did you get so good?"

Camille turned to her, flicking her chestnut-brown silky hair over her shoulder. "I was raised in Andorra," she said with a flirty shrug. "My grandparents still live there."

"How did I not know this?" Josette asked her. "And why have we not gone there?"

Camille took a sip of wine. "My grandparents have been hosting many guests the past two years." Her cheeks reddened and her eyes flicked around the table. "When things settle down, I will take you. We can go skiing."

Alonso spoke to her across me, and I shivered when his shoulder brushed mine, which he expertly noticed and apologized for, so as not to seem too familiar. They carried on in

Catalan for a few more moments, while Josette and Sasha shot me looks, and then Alonso sat back in his chair and smiled shyly at me.

"You are singer?"

I almost responded with, "Of course, and you already know that," but then I noticed the hesitant way he'd spoken, as if he truly didn't speak English.

"Uh, sí. Yo canté en el grupo. Ah, ¿cómo se dice indie rock? En Estados Unidos." I was proud of myself for my almost proficient Spanish, and I swore amusement danced in his eyes and he ran a hand over his smile. Oh, he was playing up the shy act. He may not have thought of himself as an actor, but he was *goooood*.

He crossed his arms over his chest, making his biceps pop under his tight long-sleeved white shirt. "Sing for us?" He grinned and nodded toward the stage. "Si us plau?"

My supposed allies, the French Foreign Legion, all squealed with delight and urged me on. Sasha and Josette got out of their seats and pulled me up. When the rest of the table saw what was happening, they started clapping, "Ran-dall. Ran-dall. Rand-all."

I gazed back at Alonso and his smile fell a little. Yeah, I hadn't been onstage since the night before my band quit, though no one else knew that but him. I'd told the girls the basics about the band leaving, but I hadn't gone into the whole story.

I had no doubt in my ability, but I had been shaken by the lack of confidence my band had in me as a leader when they left. Sure, it was personally motivated and not necessarily about my performance, but for me I *was* my performance, so I took it hard.

Singing in front of a group of bar patrons used to be something I thought was fun, but fear sliced through me and I almost sat back down, but Alonso's steady gaze gave me the courage to agree.

My friends and colleagues whooped and cheered for me as I made my way up to the stage and put in my name on the list. I had three people ahead of me, so I went to the bathroom to get my head on straight. For these folks, it was just karaoke, but I never took a performance lightly.

"Hey, you okay?" Ivan came in behind me. "Don't let them bully you," he said. "They tried it with me before when I first got hired. I told them I didn't sing without getting paid, and no, getting paid in liquor don't count."

I laughed. "Thanks, but I'm fine. I don't mind. It wouldn't do for me to get rusty, now would it?"

Ivan finished up in the stall and met me at the sink.

"That was some bullshit today, huh?" he asked, shaking his head. "We've had enough nationalism nonsense at home, am I right?"

"Is that what you think it is? Some sort of nationalist senti-ment? Or do you think the Catalonians are right to want to leave Spain?"

Ivan looked around to make sure we were alone and he leaned in close. "I wouldn't be discussing it out in the open, feel me? There's a lot of upset people. The Spaniards don't want to lose a fifth of their economy. The Catalonians don't want to pay more than their fair share. There's a lot of history here, and it ain't good. You saw what happened today? You saw those people out marching in the streets? This situation is a powder keg. I just hope it doesn't explode in our faces."

"Me either," I murmured, rubbing my arms, a chill breaking my skin out in goose bumps. My fingers ran over the stitching job Alonso had done in my favorite cardigan. I didn't want him to get hurt either. Whatever his assignment was, I hoped it was over with soon.

"You better get out there," Ivan said with a laugh. "Don't want to disappoint your fans."

I rolled my eyes. "Maybe next time we can do a duet?"

He nodded and his lips turned down at the corner. "I can see that. Let's see how you do tonight, though. I can't be singing with no amateur." He rubbed a finger across each eyebrow and wiggled his head. "I got a rep to protect."

I pushed him out the door. "Okay, then. Let's go."

I went back up to the stage and had one song to figure out what the hell I was going to sing. I was delighted to see the selections were vast, and the perfect song was available.

The DJ for the night called me up and gave me that funny look people get when they recognize you but aren't sure why all while my colleagues continued to cheer ridiculously loud for me.

"Senyores i senyors, aquest és el nord-americà, Randall Sutter."

I looked for Alonso, only letting my gaze land on him for a split second before the music started. I'd chosen Jeff Buckley's "Last Goodbye," and if he liked Buckley's music half as much as I did, this song would make him swoon.

My French pals squealed and the three of them pushed their way through the crowded bar to the dance floor, where they began to sway and dance to the sultry beat of the song. I took it easy on the first verse, but once I hit the chorus, I let the full power of my voice, my entire range, out to play and attempted all the dips and swerves of Buckley's incredibly vocal prowess. I kept my hands resting on the mic stand, but I couldn't keep from being moved by the lyrics. *Kiss me, please kiss me.*

My first band used to cover this song, and it was a little weird to not be playing guitar, but I didn't mind. I felt free. It was just me, no weight of a band behind me that caused me nothing but stress.

I snuck a glance at Alonso, and he was smiling broadly, his head bobbing to the music, and I wished we were alone. I pictured us lying together in his bed back in his childhood room and it gave the words more power. I didn't want that night to have been our last embrace.

The whole bar was in my thrall, and I loved it. This was why I'd become a performer in the first place. There was nothing more powerful than a rapt audience. But then Ferrer's words came back to me.

"Is this what you want? To be a music teacher?" The last words said in a tone just short of disgust.

As I looked around at my colleagues—my people—who I knew had my back, who were cheering me on, I thought, yes, right now, this is what I want.

And that was when all of the glass shattered along the front of the bar.

Screams broke out and everyone fell to the floor. Loud bangs and shouts filled the room and there was so much chaos, I froze in place, bright light blinding me. A whooshing sound filled my ears and my face grew hot, and then he was there.

"Randall, we have to move!"

Alonso grabbed my hand and dragged me into a flow of people trying to exit out the back door. I was jostled and smashed. I tripped and fell against him, but he never lost his footing. Something wet landing on my cheek, and I wiped at it. My hand came away with blood and my vasovagal response went to work, and by the time the cool night air hit my face, the edges of my vision had gone fuzzy and my skin was clammy.

"Randall?" Alonso was speaking, I knew he was, but my ears were plugged as if I had on noise-canceling headphones. He held my head in his hands and I reached up to grab his arms.

"What's happening?"

He frowned and he gestured for Ivan, speaking to him in Spanish. Ivan nodded and took over holding something against my forehead as Alonso ran back inside.

"Hold still, Randall." Ivan's voice was quiet too. Why couldn't I hear anything?

A moment later, Alonso came running back out with Lara and Josette. It appeared the whole crew from Frederick Douglass was sitting together in the parking lot behind the bar, but I didn't trust my own observation.

"Aquí. Ahora. Ayúdame."

Alonso was back with a paramedic, who started speaking but I just kept shaking my head.

"I can't Spanish right now." I patted him on the knee, and he laughed and looked up at Alonso, who was not laughing.

"No problem. What's your name?" He was cute and probably thought he was charming, but he was distracting me from who I really wanted.

"Randall. I'm...what are you doing?"

The paramedic was right in my face and every time he touched me, I winced.

"I figure since you are bleeding a lot from your forehead, I should probably stop it, don't you think?"

"Bleeding? But how?"

"Randall! Are you okay? Merde, you're bleeding." Sasha took my hand and sat beside me on the curb. "There were two explosions outside that sent glass flying into the bar. Perhaps you were hit."

"That's what it looks like to me," the paramedic said. "If he was on the stage, that's why he got cut. Higher up than everyone else and facing the glass. The bartenders were cut too."

The fact that I heard this exchange meant my hearing was coming back. If there was an explosion, that might explain why I couldn't hear very well.

I wanted Alonso, but in a moment of clarity, I knew I shouldn't ask for him. Wasn't that what spies had to do? Deal with their own boo-boos and not blow their covers?

I saw another paramedic working on Lara, and Ivan was standing with her. Josette and Sasha were holding each other...

"Where's Camille?"

Everyone looked around but she wasn't there.

Alonso, Josette, and Sasha set off in search of her, and I sat patiently while the paramedic finished butterflying the cuts on my forehead. He assured me I would have a badass scar or two to show for it.

"Do they know what happened?"

He looked around. "Unofficially? Some protestors set a police car on fire and the ammunition they had in the trunk of the car exploded. Thankfully la policía had everyone away from the car on the street, so no one out front got hurt with the exception of a police officer who got a piece of metal in his arm."

"Oh no. Is he going to be okay?"

This was getting dangerous. What if this would have happened at the school? At least it wasn't a bomb, but who knew what a mob of angry people was capable of? And which side was it? Those protestors outside were anti-independence. Who was right? Who was I to even think about making that determination?

"My head is killing me."

"You got your bell rung by that blast, probably. Thankfully, you don't need stitches. You sure you don't want to go to hospital?"

"No, no. Please. One of my friends will take me home."

"You sure? I would hate for you to be out here alone," he said, and it finally dawned on me that he was hitting on me when his hand lingered on my thigh.

As I was about to reassure him that I would be fine, around

the corner of the building came my three French pals—with Alonso. And he had his arm around Camille.

Huh. Well, he'd asked me to play along.

"Are you okay, Randall?" Camille left Alonso's side and rushed over. "I was in the bathroom when it happened! I had no idea where you all went! I've been looking for you."

She fussed over me, looking at the two bandages I had on my forehead. God, I hoped the scars weren't too bad. They seemed huge, as it had taken him forever to patch me up.

"Alonso is going to give us a ride back," Josette said, brushing my hair back.

"¿Puedes caminar?" Alonso held out his arm in case I needed support.

"I'm okay. Thank you."

I stood and smiled at him, but he simply nodded and gestured for the women to walk ahead of him. I followed the group out of the parking lot, still feeling pretty dazed. Alonso had parked four blocks away, which was good in that we didn't have to navigate the still gathered people in the square in front of the bar. The police were dispersing the crowd, but there were still a few folks chanting.

I was yawning by the time we got to Alonso's car and didn't move quick enough. Camille took shotgun, forcing me into the middle of the backseat between Sasha and Josette. I was too tired to think much about Camille's hand on Alonso's arm or his knee, but it did help when he caught my eye in the rearview mirror a couple of times.

We got to our complex and Camille invited us all up to their place.

"I need sleep, but thank you. I want to get out of these bloody clothes and go to bed."

I got air kisses from the girls, who tried to fuss over me some more, but I insisted they go have fun with their new friend. I winked at them and went inside my place. All I had the energy to do was take ibuprofen and drink a glass of water before I stripped off my clothes, leaving them in the middle of the flat to wash the next day. I was headed into the bathroom when movement caught my eye on my back patio.

I jumped and nearly screamed before I realized it was Alonso.

I was too tired to even worry about only being in my boxers. I opened the door for him and he took me in his arms.

"I was so worried, amor." He kissed me, and I was about to melt in his arms when I realized how gross I was.

"Let me shower, please. I'm covered in blood and who knows what else."

He tilted his head and carefully lifted my hair off of my forehead. "You need to keep this dry," he said. "Let me wash you."

ELEVEN

AFTER MIDNIGHT SATURDAY, Castelldefels, Catalonia, Spain

I must have been too tired to argue because I found myself in the tiny shower, holding a towel over my face while Alonso carefully washed my hair, using the handheld nozzle to keep my cuts from getting wet. It helped to be able to hide my face, helped me not think about him seeing all of me. I'd only done this once before, with Rig. And directly after he and I had gotten out of the shower and were drying off, he'd mentioned us joining a gym together, or maybe going running more often.

Message received. Loud and clear.

Alonso's first words after he finished with my hair?

"Let me in, amor. I want to take care of you."

I did. And he did. He stripped down to his boxers and squeezed into the stall with me. I tried not to think about the fact that I was naked in front of him with the lights on. When I tried to protest, he shushed me. He washed me all over, and then, instead of turning it into an opportunity to grope me or make it sexual, he held me tight to him under the hot spray, keeping the wadded-up towel to my face so my cuts wouldn't get wet.

"I hate that you got hurt," he finally said, and I realized that this care session was as much about his needs as it was about mine.

"Did you like your song?" I asked him, moving the towel so I could peek at him.

"I loved my song," he breathed, and his dark red lips split into a tender smile. "You sing so beautifully."

"Well, thanks, but what are you doing here? I thought you'd gone home with Camille." I wiggled my eyebrows, but that made me wince, and he rolled his eyes, shutting off the water. He reached out and grabbed my last two towels stacked on the shelf in the corner. "They had a bet going, you know. Who you'd like better."

"You know who I like," he said, his voice gravelly, and he wrapped me in a towel. "It would not have been a fair bet."

"Yeah, but I didn't know what you would do, remember? Maybe your cover was being a dude bro who was after the hot French chicks."

He pulled me against him and grabbed my ass. "Is that why you sang for me? Trying to tip the scales in your favor?"

I gaped at him and swatted at his chest. "I'll have you know they pushed me to go up there. It was all their idea."

He cupped my jaw and kissed me gently. "But you chose Jeff Buckley."

Okay, he had me there. "Did it work?"

"What do you think?" He kissed me again, but then he looked up at my forehead and frowned. "We need to get you to bed."

I pulled back. Maybe the shower had doused his attraction after all.

"I'm fine." I pulled the towel tighter around my chest and moved past him to the bedroom. My face was hot, my forehead stung, and what little bit of pride I had was wounded.

Alonso fastened his towel around his waist, slid off his wet boxers, and followed me.

"Randall, what is wrong? Have I said something?"

I paused. I was being stupid. "No, sorry. I'm feeling a little overwhelmed tonight."

"Of course you are. You were in an explosion. You need rest." He looked at me with his head tilted and he narrowed his eyes. "But it's something else, isn't it?"

"I love that you take care of me, that you came here tonight. I'm just not good at reading the room. I'm afraid my last relationship has me worrying about things."

He planted his hands on his hips, and sighed. "I am here because I want you. Not because you sang for me, not because of my job, and not because of any sort of obligation. You are the most beautiful man I've ever seen, Randall. I'm here because you are a bright spot in a time that could be very dark for me. You see me when others haven't, and you never ask anything of me. And despite what you think, I see you too. I see what you try to hide. I don't *want* you to hide. Let me see all of you, amor. I want all of you, whatever you want to give me."

"God, I'm trying not to cry over here. Stop," I said, but I laughed as my eyes welled up.

He moved across the room and took me in his arms, burying his face in my neck. I felt him take a big breath and let it out. "Can I stay? I want to hold you."

"That sounds terrible." I smiled so wide my cheeks hurt. "I'll hate every minute of it."

I crawled into bed and then dropped the towel on the floor. "Do you want some sweats or something?"

"Is it okay that I don't?"

I held up the blanket. "Very."

There was something very comforting about Alonso's presence, and I slept soundly for the first time in a long time. I still woke at daybreak, however, as my body was on a pretty regular schedule.

Alonso was still asleep, pressed against my back, his arm draped over my side, his other arm under my pillow. I wanted to roll over and watch him, but if I moved at all, he tightened his grip with a grunt. I loved it. But then he shifted, and I felt his hard dick against my ass.

Oh hello.

"You are squirmy in the morning," he said, his lips brushing the back of my neck.

"I wanted to be creepy and watch you sleep."

"I like you like this," he said, and he shifted his hips. His erection slid between my legs, and I gasped.

"I like *you* like this," I said, pushing my hips back against him.

He moaned and thrust against me, sliding his erection over my sensitive skin, past my balls, and brushing the base of my cock.

"Can I touch you? Can I make you feel good, amor?"

"Yes. Please. *Si us plau.*"

He chuckled against my neck and nuzzled against my hair.

And he made me feel *so* good. The pressure, the friction, was so intense, and when he licked his palm and stroked my already leaking cock, I was in heaven. He held me so tight, with one hand splayed on my chest and the other stroking me in synch with his thrusts, his slow, full-bodied thrusts that had my whole body trembling.

I loved being surrounded by him, possessed by him. I squeezed my thighs together, hooking my ankles, and Alonso moaned louder, muttering something in Catalan that sounded spicy. I reached back and grabbed his hip, pulling him even closer as I felt the telltale rush of heat that meant I was close...so close.

"I'm gonna come, baby," I said. "I'm gonna...I'm... *Ohhhhh.*"

"El meu cor, Randall." And I felt the warmth of his spend coat my thighs as his whole body shuddered. His movements slowed and he pressed kisses and nibbles into my shoulder.

"Best morning ever," I said, turning enough to kiss his lips.

He grabbed his towel that he'd left on his side of the bed the night before, and cleaned us up, finally allowing me to roll over and wrap myself around him.

"I'm afraid I need to leave, though," he said, running his hands over my back. "I don't want to move, but I can't chance being seen here, and I know where my cousin has cameras." He kissed me and then climbed out of bed. "Can I come back tonight?"

"Si us plau. See? I practiced." I stretched my arms above my head and basked in the warm feeling and the beautiful view of Alonso walking around my flat naked, in search of his clothes from the night before.

He pulled on his jeans sans undies, as they were still wet from our shower. How thoughtful of him to have done that, to let me know that the shower was not for his sexual gratification. He had been so respectful of me, never pushing for more than I was ready to give him.

"I didn't even ask...did you find out anything about last night?"

He shook his head. "No, but I'm going to call my

commander this morning." He tugged on his shirt and slid his feet into his boots. "He wants...*hostia*, I don't like this. He wants us to go together to Ferrer's next weekend."

I sat up in bed. "Really? Okay. So I should RSVP like he asked?"

"Sí. You will need a suit if you don't own one. From what my sources say, this gathering he is having is meant to be a fundraiser for the separatists under the guise of raising money to pay the legal fees of those arrested after the referendum, but we believe they are actually raising money for something else. I can't tell you more than that, but these are dangerous people, Randall. Don't forget that."

"I won't. But what name should I put for you?"

He grinned. "Alonso Rey."

"King?" I laughed, and he held his hands out. "More like Alonso Dios," I joked, and his cheeks flushed. "Come here, king, so I can kiss you once before you disappear."

He knelt beside the bed and he led the kiss. When he pulled back, he examined the bandages on my forehead. "He did a decent job, but you might have a scar, amor. Lo siento."

I shrugged. "As long as you still kiss me like that, I don't care."

That got me one more kiss.

"Stay in today? If you can. At least don't go off alone. There may be more protests. Last night was a fluke, I think. But I don't want to take a chance with you. And there will be more security around the school next week, Lara said. More parents have hired security for their children."

"What do you think will end this? Seems an impossible situation."

Alonso ran a hand through his curls. "No sé. I can only hope to stop something worse from happening." He gave me a sad smile. "Stay safe. Get some rest. I'll be back after dark tonight."

"*You* be safe," I said, because even though he was the expert in this situation, I would worry for him.

"Siempre, claro. Bon dia, amor."

He blew me a kiss and walked out onto my balcony, climbing over the side.

Leaving me a whole day to...worry. And wait for Alonso to come back and hold me.

TWELVE

I RSVP'd to the Ferrers' gathering, and then set to freaking out for the rest of the day. When he arrived late that evening, Alonso convinced me to have the girls take me shopping one day after school for a suit.

"Guess my cardigan isn't fancy enough?"

We lay on the couch together in my flat watching a Jason Bourne film with the sound off and some soft piano music playing through my Bluetooth speaker. I was in my favorite cardigan and boxers. Alonso was gloriously naked and wrapped in a blanket like the gift that he was.

"I love that you mended it for me. Where did you learn to sew?"

"In the army. You tear your trousers enough times, you learn or your ass hangs out." He fingered the collar of my sweater. "I see why you like this sweater so much. I love the color on you."

"Thank you," I said, kissing him. "I wore it for our first show after we signed with our label and it went so well, I decided it was my lucky sweater. Over the years it became like my security blanket. I was so grateful I had it on when we got robbed or it would have been gone too."

"You lost your instruments. Did they have sentimental meaning for you?"

"Yeah. My laptop had a lot of music on it that I'd recorded, songs in various stages of being finished. My three electric guitars and an acoustic guitar, plus my personal amp and head, my rack system and pedals. The acoustic was my first guitar, the one I learned how to play on. I played it at every show. Kinda felt like losing a limb."

Alonso frowned off into the distance and ran a hand over his head, back and forth. "Have you gone to look at purchasing a new one?"

I shook my head and reached for his hand. I loved to trace the fine lines and veins, and it usually got him to relax. Sure enough, he sank back into the arm of the couch and pulled me closer, snuggled against his chest.

"I haven't been back to Barcelona proper since I moved out here. It's not on my list of necessities. The students who are studying guitar with me have their own, and there was a beat-up guitar in a closet that I can at least use to demonstrate how to fret but...there are more important things to worry about right now."

Alonso lifted my chin into look in my eyes. "When my assignment is over, I would love to take you guitar shopping. Would you let me?"

I would let him take me anywhere. He made me feel incredibly safe. It was hard to think about the fact that we were in the middle of civil unrest all around us when we were wrapped in each other's arms.

"Well, you know. If you have time. I don't even know...what do you do when you aren't being the Spanish Jason Bourne?"

He barked out a laugh and glanced at the screen. Bourne was fighting some guy in a tiny bathroom to the soothing sounds of Hozier in the background.

"When I am not on duty or deployed somewhere, I work at the winery. In fact, the place is due for a complete refresh of cameras and computers, so when I'm done with this situation, I'll be back working for my father and brother." He shrugged. "It should be less stressful. Perhaps. I am not sure how it will be working under my baby brother. I will have to rein in my need to mess with him."

I rolled onto my stomach so I could see him clearly, perhaps get a read on his thoughts. "Do you see a possibility that we might...date each other?" My stomach dropped thinking I wasn't sure if I wanted to know the answer.

Alonso grinned and curled a lock of my hair around his finger. "Is that what we are doing?"

I blinked at him. "Is that...what you want?"

He narrowed his eyes and exhaled. "No."

I pushed up, ready to scramble away, when he tangled his legs with mine, forcing me down on top of him with some move he probably learned to fight off bad guys.

"No, amor. I don't want to *date* you. I want to *love* you."

It took a moment for his words to sink in.

"*Oh.*"

"*Sí,*" he said as he brushed my hair back with one hand and ran his other over my ass. "Dating is too casual an arrangement for how I feel for you."

My cheeks roared with heat and I dipped my gaze, tracing a finger in his chest hair. He was so touchable with all that soft, curly hair. I couldn't get enough of touching him.

"For me too, but I didn't want to assume."

"Si us plau, amor. Please assume."

I smiled as he lifted his head to kiss me lazily, licking at my lips and tongue in teasing strokes until my whole body thrummed with need.

"And...your family? They will not object?"

He shrugged. "Papa, he will be confused. Mama will first be disappointed about perhaps no grandbabies and then happy be for me. Felip will tease me for robbing the cradle. Tomás will have his suspicions confirmed. And Mateu? I don't know. I assume he will be happy, but he is tough to predict, that one." He nibbled at my chin. "And your family?"

I laughed. "Not surprised at all. I've been out to my family since I was seventeen and finally had an interest in something other than music. I was a late bloomer. My family didn't think it was a big deal. My father's brother is gay and everyone accepted him from day one." I deflated a little. "Of course, they won't know unless I call them. At some point, I guess, I'm going to have to be the one to suck it up and reach out."

Alonso understood, I knew he would somehow.

"You have to decide, is it worth it to be right or to be loved, eh?"

"Exactly. You get me."

"I *want* you, amor. Let me have you."

And I did. I let him have his way with me, and I didn't even care that I was naked in the middle of my living room with the lights still on.

But my take-on-the-world attitude faded Monday when I received an email from Mr. Ferrer.

Bon dia, senyor Sutter. Delighted you will be joining us for our gala this weekend. I would very much like for you to accompany Pere on this surprise he has for me. I think it will give him a little reassurance to know you are there beside him. Then I would love for you to play a song with me. Since you do not play in my style, and I am unfamiliar with your music, how about we play a song that we can both connect with? Here are some suggestions for you to learn. We can decide on Friday when I pick up Pere from school? Does that work for you? My guests are thrilled you will be joining us for this important event. Gràcies, professor.

"You could almost think he was a good man," Lara said when I showed it to her Tuesday afternoon. "As for the songs... Jose Feliciano? I suppose that's a choice. 'Malagueña' I get, it's a beautiful song. Julio Iglesias, though? He's not Catalan even." She shook her head. "What do you feel comfortable with?"

"None of it, honestly, but I want to play with Pere, especially if it makes him feel better. I asked him, and he seemed relieved. I've already started working on the tablature. I'll have to use the guitar he left, as I don't have one. It shouldn't be a problem to learn the other songs. If I refuse, I'll look like the asshole, and that sucks."

"What can I do to help?"

"I don't know, send me positive vibes? My stomach is already a wreck. I'll probably be a mess by Friday. Thankfully Josette and Sasha took me to a great tailor yesterday. He took my measurements and promised to do a rush job on a suit for me. I'm getting fitted Thursday and he said it would be ready by Saturday."

That trip had been a lot better than I'd thought. I'd lost a little weight and a size thirty-eight waist fit me comfortably. Josette talked me into a royal blue vest to match the suit, which did wonders for my shape, and we found a perfect shirt. I went with a bright gold tie and planned to wear a red pocket square with gold flowers on it. I rounded out the outfit with new brown derby shoes and matching belt. I hadn't dressed up like this since the first Grammy awards we'd attended two years prior.

Alonso had approved and said he would be dressed to kill. He might have meant literally.

Lara squeezed my hand, bringing me back to the conversation. "You'll be great. And Alonso is going with you?" She raised her eyebrows and smiled.

My face got hot. "Yes, he's...Lara, I don't like keeping things from you, but we're sort of..."

She burst out laughing and grabbed for my hand. "Oh my God, Randall, that's wonderful!"

"But I know it's against the rules—"

"It would be if he were actually my employee, which he's not. And I know it's a rule, but I also know there are others hooking up on this campus, with each other and with people in the community. Don't even worry about it." She leaned forward over the desk and stage whispered, "He's so hot, I don't know how you could possibly keep your hands to yourself."

I put a hand over my mouth and looked to the ceiling.

"Okay, okay. Let's pretend I know nothing. Let me know if I can help with the thing Saturday, and Randall...be careful. I don't like this at all. Alonso doesn't either, but he has promised me that you'll be safe."

"I trust him, Lara. I'll be careful. I don't know what's going on with these people, but I hate for Pere to be in the middle of it all. That little boy is just the sweetest."

"He really is."

She filled me in on a few other people she assumed would be there, important people in the Castelldefels community at large, including several fútbol players and politicians. I thanked her and then headed back to my classroom to get to work learning these songs. No problem. Four songs by Friday. Easy-peasy.

. . .

"Well, Mr. Rock Star, what song did you choose?"

He'd shown up on time to pick up Pere Friday afternoon, and even flashed me his ID before walking into the room.

I smiled more confidently than I felt. "Any of them are fine with me."

He put an arm around Pere and raised his eyebrows. "Well, then. How about we let the guests decide tomorrow?"

"Sounds good." I would definitely be practicing until my fingers fell off tonight, probably wouldn't sleep, and would likely be spending a lot of time in the bathroom, but he didn't need to know that.

"And your...friend? Date? Will be there tomorrow by seven o'clock, sí?"

"Si és clar. Looking forward to it." *Looking forward to this being all over, anyway.*

"Bé. Pere, get your things, let's let senyor Sutter get home to rest."

"Pere, remember what I told you," I said, giving him a wink.

We'd spent lunch the past three days and a large portion of his lesson today talking about how to keep your cool when performing in front of others, how to recover if you make a mistake, and how the performance isn't just about your technical playing but how you put your heart into your music.

"No matter what happens tomorrow," I'd said to him, but it was as much for me as for him, "you know you did your best, you tried your hardest, and your father knows this. Most importantly, I want you to be proud of yourself, verdad?"

"Sí, senyor Sutter. I want him to be proud of me too."

I took a deep breath. I had to keep my feelings about the man, and fathers in general, to myself.

"Parents can't help but be proud of their kids when they see them shine, and you shine brighter than any star in the sky. ¿Me entiendes?"

"Sí. You're doing pretty good too."

I barked out a laugh. "Why, thank you, Pere." I gave him a fist bump and he giggled. We'd practiced the song several times before his father arrived, and with the exception of a couple of bumpy transitions, he was playing it great. And not just great for a ten-year-old. Great for a beginning pianist at any age.

"See you tomorrow," I said to them both, and as they walked outside, I collapsed against the table and let out a big breath.

I hoped that whatever happened tomorrow night, Pere was safe, and Alonso was one step closer to being done with this assignment.

I thought back to the incident at the bar and how that explosion could have done more than cut up my face and injure a police officer. Someone could have been killed, and until the issue of Catalonia's independence was settled, protests and violence could crop up at any time. Based on what I knew, I couldn't speculate on which option would be best for the country or the people, but I knew that this precarious situation needed to be resolved before more people got hurt.

I packed up my things, including Ferrer's guitar, and I walked home, distracted. I nearly stepped wrong off the curb and thought how awesome that would be to either break the guitar or myself.

I made it to my apartment unscathed and texted Josette that I wouldn't be coming to Friday Social, as I needed to prepare for the event the following evening.

Take care, mon frère, was her response. *We go to pick up your suit at 10.*

I set the guitar case on my dinette and stepped back from it. It felt weird having it in my flat. I was still staring at it when Alonso knocked on the patio door.

I let him in and he took me in his arms, kissing me gently.

"¿Estás preocupado?"

I told him I was worried. We sat together at the table, looking at the case.

"Do you think it will bite you?" he finally asked, and it was enough to get me out of my mood.

"Maybe," I said.

He stood and pulled two food containers and a small white box out of his backpack and set them on the counter.

"I cooked for us. I knew you wouldn't be up to going out and that you don't have much here to cook with." He raised an eyebrow at me and I gave him a look back. This was not the night to judge my culinary situation.

He opened one of the containers and filled two of my second-hand bowls with paella that smelled wonderful. The other container and the white box he put in the fridge.

"You are a fabulous cook," I said with a happy sigh. I hadn't eaten well all week. "Is there anything you can't do?"

He nodded as he took a bite and thought for a moment. "I can't sing or play guitar."

I rolled my eyes. "Those are hardly useful skills."

He tapped on his chin, his finger touching his dimple. I loved that dimple. "Then you are right. I can do everything."

I barked out a laugh and hooked my leg over his. I recalled what Camille said about his cleaning skills and I figured I wouldn't bring that up. I could clean just fine for the both of us.

After we ate his delicious food and drank a bottle of his favorite wine from the family vineyard, he sat with me while I played through the three songs Ferrer had picked, as well as the song Pere had prepared to play. When I finished, I was surprisingly relaxed. The wine must have done the trick.

"It's amazing. You can just play those songs after a few days."

I set the guitar in the case, figuring I'd prepared as much as I could. "Well, a few days, and years and years of practice. I can sight read, but it's always better to be prepared."

"Will he have you sing?"

I shrugged. "I can if he asks. I don't want this man to have a leg up on me."

Alonso's brow furrowed. "He cannot compare to you. I don't care how well he plays guitar or sings."

I held my hands against my heart. "Of all the men to fall on in Barcelona, I'm so happy it was you."

He rolled his eyes at my pretend swoon and took my hand. "Let's get some rest. I want you aware and alert tomorrow. I will be with you the whole time, but if anything happens…"

"Are you worried?"

He shook his head but it wasn't definitive. "Not really? I anticipate it will be a house full of wealthy, influential people who will be throwing their money around to gain favor. Potentially there will be some inflammatory statements made, but I hope I will have a clearer picture of who the players are." He frowned. "Randall, promise me, if anything goes wrong, you will leave. I will show you a rendezvous point on our way in and if anything happens, you run straight there. I will have a member of our unit there for backup, but I don't want to have to call them."

"Yeah, of course I will, but what could actually happen?"

I should have known better than to even voice that thought.

Because the shitstorm started twenty minutes later.

Alonso had gotten me into bed and feeling nice and relaxed, ready for a good night's sleep, when his phone rang.

"Mama. ¿Qué ha pasado?"

I heard her speaking in Catalan through the phone, her voice thick and shaky from her tears. I held Alonso's hand as he listened carefully, squeezing every so often when she grew particularly emotional and her voice rose in pitch.

"I'm coming now. Go with Mateu. I'll meet you at hospital. Sit down until I get there. T'estimo, Mama." He disconnected the call and ran his hand through his hair.

"What can I do?"

He turned to face me with a scowl. "Say you will stay here. Lock the door. I need to go. My cover is blown."

"Your cover?"

He stood from the bed and looked around for his boots. "My father had uninvited guests at the winery today. Turned out they were pro-independencia and they had an argument. After they left, my father had chest pains, so Mama called an ambulance. He had a heart attack twelve years ago and had to mostly retire from the winery, that is why first Felip and now Mateu are running the business, and why my family wants me there more often. I should have been there."

"But how does this mean your cover is blown?" I didn't want him going into a dangerous situation, though I knew he would immediately go to his family no matter what.

"One of them recognized me in a picture on the wall and asked why, if things were so good at Cava Segura, was his son working as a custodian at the international school." He put on his coat and grabbed his backpack. "Has to be someone from the school. She did not know these men."

I climbed from the bed and wrapped my cardigan around myself. "I'm so sorry, Alonso. Do you want me to come with you?"

He shook his head and looked down at his feet. "I need to see to my family. I'm going to call my commander and tell him you aren't going tomorrow."

"Wait, Alonso." I placed a hand on his arm, feeling the tension flowing through him. "I have to go tomorrow."

He scowled at me. "Not without me. It's not safe."

I promptly removed my hand from him and raised my eyebrows, but I kept my voice gentle. "I have to go. For Pere. For all the kids who are in danger from these people fighting at their school. This is your state, your country, so I understand that you are involved, but this has become my community, and I need to do what I can to help. You said you'd have a colleague outside? Well, is there someone else who could go as my date?"

I didn't think his scowl could get deeper.

"You know what? You go check on your family. We can talk tomorrow."

He exhaled and nodded, but wouldn't make eye contact with me.

Until he did.

And his gaze was that of a man who was on his last gasp of control.

"Hey," I said, cupping his jaw, running my thumb over his dimple, which the more I studied the dip there, it was uneven, almost like a scar. "It's going to be okay."

He squeezed his eyes shut, nodded, and stepped away from me. He walked toward the front door—the first time he wasn't sneaking in or out—and placed his hand on the knob. I suppose he didn't care who saw him leave in his current state of mind.

When he didn't speak, I walked toward him and placed a hand on his back. I got the desired response when he turned and took me in his arms with a big sigh.

"Si us plau, amor. Ves amb compte."

I could gather what that meant.

"I promise." The rush of affection I felt for this man overwhelmed any fear I had for my own safety. "I wish I could take care of you for once."

He stepped back and brushed a quick kiss across my lips. "You do. You have. You will."

I should have gone with him. I should have insisted, but who was I to barge in on his family right now? I just hoped he would reach out to me when he was able.

I didn't sleep much, and when I did, it was filled with anxious dreams. Sounds like power tools became a grinding pain in my head. Heart-pounding scenes of running with only the sound of my heavy breathing in my ears. Standing in a crowd of shouting protestors, but instead of chanting and fists punched to the sky, they turned their vitriol on me.

By six in the morning I couldn't take it anymore. I was ready to climb out of my skin. I checked my phone and found a text from Alonso from hours earlier.

Papa is home resting. No heart attack. Tests were okay.

I was relieved and grateful that he'd let me know.

I texted back, *Thank you. Get some rest. We can talk when you are able.*

I couldn't stand to be in my flat a moment longer.

I dressed in warm clothes and tucked my hair up in a beanie, locked the door, and started walking. I hadn't been to the beach in a few weeks, and I thought maybe watching the sun rise might give me some perspective. It took me about thirty minutes to get there, and the sky did not disappoint. I wasn't one of those yoga-at-daybreak kind of folks, but feeling the sun on my face, watching the light dance on the waves, it loosened some of the tension I'd been holding onto. The cool breeze cleansed me of the panic from my dreams and I found a bit of clarity.

I knew I needed to go to Ferrer's. I had to do my part, though I knew this was a miniscule portion of a larger problem. If I didn't go, whatever occurred afterward would have a profound impact on me and the people I'd grown to care about.

I'd already survived the explosion at the bar. I had to follow through, and it wasn't just my ego not wanting Ferrer to have sway over me.

I would share my location with Alonso and Lara, I would leave if anything happened, and I would stay only as long as I needed to make an appearance. It would be fine.

I passed a panaderia on the way home and stopped to pick up some muffins, coffee, and fruit to take back with me so I'd have some food for later. When I opened my fridge, I spotted the white box Alonso had brought the night before. I pulled it out, slid a finger under the lid to break the tape, and opened the box.

Inside was a yellow rose boutonniere. It wasn't fussy, but it was quite fragrant. I took it out of the tissue paper and examined the pearl-tipped pin that would be used to fasten it—and noticed a tiny device that resembled some sort of chip was implanted in the tip. Perhaps this was how Alonso planned to have the situation monitored at the party? Okay, well, I'd wear it then. I could do this. I could be brave for him, for the kids.

Josette came to see me at ten to go with me to pick up my suit, so we took a cab. She took loads of pictures of me in the full getup, made me pose like a supermodel and everything.

"Who knows? One of these might be the cover artwork for your next album."

I frowned. "If there is a next album."

She hip-checked me. "Randall, you can't possibly think your music career is over. Sure, your band is over, but you don't need them. I am a witness. I heard you sing. I saw what you can do to a roomful of people with that voice of yours. Alonso wasn't even paying attention to Camille," she said with a conspiratorial laugh. "That's why she went to the bathroom. She was disappointed."

I feigned shock and she laughed even louder. I wondered

what she'd say if she would have seen Alonso leaving my flat the previous night.

I returned home with plans to shower, blow out my hair and paint my nails, but when I opened the door to my flat, there were two men in military uniforms inside my flat.

"Please don't be alarmed," one of them said, raising a hand. "I am Comandante Luis Costa. I am Sargento Segura's commanding officer." He pulled out his ID, I'm sure because I was hovering in the doorway like I might bolt.

"What are you doing here?"

Costa nodded toward the other man, who stood and gave a slight bow.

"This is Cabo Carlos Ruiz. He will be going with you as Alonso Rey with you to the Ferrer's gathering tonight in place of Sargento Segura."

"Does, um, Sergeant Segura know about this?"

"Sargento Segura has been removed from this assignment," the commander said.

"Because of what happened with his family?"

He gave a curt nod. "In part. Now, we need to prepare you for this evening's gala."

I was given a few moments to hang up my suit, partake of some of the paella Alonso had left since I hadn't had lunch, although it went down like sawdust. I had no idea how to act with these men in my home, and all I cared about was whether Alonso was okay. I hoped he hadn't gotten in trouble for staying with me. Did they know we were involved?

Once I sat down across from the commander, he smiled jovially. He was probably mid-thirties, about the same age as Alonso, I figured, and Ruiz was younger. Ruiz was handsome in that clean-cut, man-in-uniform kind of way. Our cover story was that we'd met in Barcelona at the Picasso Museum before I moved to Castelldefels, and we had been out on a few occasions but we were keeping it casual. Ruiz was supposed to be an art student attending Escola Massana, and that he was originally from Sitges, a place I hadn't been yet but planned to visit soon.

"If you get confused or rattled," Costa said, "simply look to Ruiz to answer. He can convince your àvia—your grandmother—he is the pope, can't you, Ruiz?"

The soldier smirked and bowed his head. "I live to serve."

While these two seemed capable enough, they also didn't seem to be taking this as seriously as Alonso had.

"Moreover, Ruiz will be able to explain how his family was in favor of the referendum and his parents supported the former president in exile, Carles Puigdemont. These are details that will put the others at ease speaking around him. I don't expect anything of major importance to come from this but we have to cover all of the bases, as you say in America." He chuckled and typed a few things into his laptop.

"Well, I'm glad he will be there. I don't know very much about the independence movement," I admitted.

"And why would you? It will be fine, just let Ruiz do the talking," Costa said. "It will be just as Sargento Segura told you. We will be monitoring you from a safe position, which Ruiz will point out on your way into the Ferrer property. If he tells you to go, you go. ¿Me entiendes?"

"Sí," I said. "Is there anything you want me to look for? Anything I should do?"

"No, gràcies. You shall entertain, speak to whomever asks to speak to you, and when it seems appropriate, Ruiz will collect you and you will say your goodbyes. This is not to be a lengthy visit. We will have people outside collecting information on the other guests. If Ruiz thinks there is danger, he will say that his mother phoned and she is not well."

"And what if *I* feel there is a problem?"

Costa tilted his head. "I know you have no family here. Is there a friend?"

"Yes, uh, I can say Josette called, and she's not well?"

"That will be fine. Josette. You catch that Ruiz?"

"Sí, és clar."

"Bé." He looked at his watch. "I suppose the two of you should get ready."

"I'm going to shower," I said, leaving them to their discussion. I didn't love having strangers in my house while I showered, but what else could I do? I took my time in the hopes I could get my nerves under control. I did indeed blow out my hair and painted my nails a shimmery gold to match my tie. I wandered back out to my kitchen and was waiting for them to dry when I caught a screen of pictures up on Costa's computer.

"Wait, I know him."

They turned to look at me and I pointed at the screen. "That man has come to school with Mr. Ferrer a few times. They approached people together. And that man," I said, recognizing one of the drivers. "I think he works for Mr. Vidal. He's been at the school with him. And that man, he has a student in my afternoon class. He's come in to pick the child up before."

"These are all persons of interest in our investigation. None of them are of too much concern. I am only giving you this information in order for you to perhaps listen a little more carefully when they are speaking, or perhaps to even stand near to them tonight, if it seems proper."

Somehow I didn't think Alonso would agree to this, so I made a mental note to be extra cautious around those people, not attempt to get closer. The more he spoke, the more Costa seemed as if he was just going through the motions and this was just another routine mission, nothing more. It sure didn't feel that way to me.

I've always been a big reader, and cozy mysteries are a lot of fun, but I had no intention of putting myself in the damsel-in-distress role, nor the amateur sleuth. No. I wanted peace at my school. That was it.

"Mind if I go change?" Ruiz held up a garment bag, and I gestured toward the bathroom.

"Be my guest."

Costa stopped him. "If the two of you are supposed to be casually dating, there is an expectation that you may be physically affectionate with each other."

Ruiz and I looked at each other. He grinned.

"Not a problem for me. I get to be the pretend boyfriend to an American rock star."

"Um...I'm okay with a hand to the back or a kiss on the cheek," I said. "That's about as much as I would ever do with anyone in public, no matter how long we'd been together." I didn't want this guy all over me, nor did I want him taking liberties. The only one I wanted to touch me couldn't be there and this guy was no substitute.

Ruiz shrugged. "Understood. Maybe I will have my picture taken with you and gain more Instagram followers." He winked and then laughed. "I'm joking. I will go get dressed."

He slung the garment bag over his shoulder and strolled into the bathroom, shutting the door behind him.

"He will act appropriately, you have my word," the commander said. "Ruiz is young, but he is a good soldier and has done this work before."

I sighed. That wasn't building up my confidence, but again, I wasn't heading into a den of arms dealers or a drug cartel compound. This was a party at the home of a popular Catalan musician, where at least one child would be present.

I almost thought to myself, how bad could it...

• • •

We pulled up to the Ferrers' house at 6:55 p.m. in a nondescript black sedan—I didn't even know what make or model the car was—after Ruiz showed me where the rendezvous point was around the corner. In case of emergency, I was to go to a van there, where Costa and another officer would be monitoring what the listening devices we were wearing picked up.

"If anything goes wrong, we will call in la policía as backup. Don't worry. You will be safe."

It seemed simple enough, the entire scenario.

Tell that to my integumentary system.

I was sweating profusely down my back. I prayed the undershirt, dress shirt, and vest would be enough material to absorb it and I wouldn't have sweat stains showing by the time we were meant to play.

Costa touched my back as we were walking in, and when I flinched, he whispered, "You can't do that around other people if we're going to pull this off."

"I'm sorry, I know. I'm just...I'm fucking nervous. I'm sweating like a pig, all down my back." I adjusted my grip on the guitar case, which was slipping around in my sweaty palm. *Jesus.*

He smiled down at me—he was at least six inches taller than me and was fit like Alonso, but bulkier. "You will be safe. As long as you don't ramble nervously, you will be fine. Just pretend like you don't know anything—which you don't—and let them bury themselves. These wealthy assholes think nothing can touch them. They'd send us all back to the stone age for their pride."

"This is personal for you?" I asked.

"Sí. Jo sóc catalá. Yo soy de España. Es lo mismo. ¿Me entiendes? They are one and the same. Catalunya is part of the whole of España and stronger because of that."

I nodded. "Thank you. I appreciate you telling me that."

As we approached the door, he leaned down and kissed my cheek. This time I didn't flinch. He didn't smell good like Alonso, nor did I feel attracted to him at all, but he was doing his job, and that meant he would protect me. I had to trust him and Costa.

"We are being watched," he whispered in my ear.

I smiled up at him, though I was sure it didn't reach my eyes.

The door opened and I stood straighter.

"Bona nit. You must be senyor Sutter. I've heard so much about you."

I held out my hand to shake. "Senyora Ferrer," I said, recognizing Pere's stepmother. "Yes, I'm Randall Sutter, and this is my date, Alonso." I hoped I hadn't made a face when I gave Alonso's name. Carlos Ruiz certainly was not *my* Alonso.

My Alonso. God, I missed him. I hated not knowing if he was okay. But I had to push the worry out of my mind or I'd blow this whole thing.

"Call me Doriana," she said, seeming less like the stepmonster I'd imagined her to be. Perhaps she was an excellent host and actress, but not necessarily the best parent. That could definitely be the case.

Ruiz took her hand, spoke to her in Catalan and kissed her cheeks.

"Molt de gust," she said and gestured for us to enter. "Randall, Paolo would like to see you for a few minutes in his study. Jaume will escort you." She reached for the arm of a large suited gentleman, who I recognized as Ferrer's driver. "Alonso, how about you come with me to the bar?"

And so we were already to be separated. Ruiz glanced at me, his smile only slightly slipping, and he nodded to me, taking Doriana's arm. The two of them chatted in Catalan and he definitely played the part of the gay love interest, turning back to smile at me.

What he *wasn't* playing was the protective undercover soldier, and that had me on edge.

"This way," the big man said, pointing to the left of the foyer. The place was a mansion. The foyer had a huge domed roof with skylights and there was a mural on the ceiling of clouds and angels, similar to but not exactly like any I'd seen before. I wondered how old the place was. Had Ferrer's family lived here long, or had he purchased the place with earnings from his illustrious career?

Try as I might to appreciate the aesthetic, I had to focus my energy on not vomiting.

I heard male laughter as Jaume pushed open the door and announced us.

"Ah, welcome, Randall. Gentlemen, we have a real American rock star with us tonight."

Here we go. I kicked my chin out and pretended like these men were just like the tech bros we'd played for in private gigs after we'd won our Grammy. They had to posture to make themselves feel better. Some of that, "Oh I played in a band in college," or "I used to play but I had bigger things to do with my life" blah blah. It wasn't worth it to get competitive or take any of their jabs personally.

"Yes, sir. Here and ready to play."

He came over and shook my hand. "Let me introduce you to some of my guests. This is Ambròs Vidal, who you may have met at Frederick Douglass."

I shook hands with the man, who had a super intense gaze. He nodded at me, but did not smile.

Ferrer then introduced two music producers, an FC Barcelona fútbol player and his bodyguard, and an older man who was an art dealer.

"Molt de gust. I appreciate the invitation."

Ferrer put a hand on my shoulder. "We are happy you are here and are looking forward to hearing what my boy has been working on as well. But we also wanted to speak to you about the purpose for tonight's gathering, so you are not taken by surprise."

Vidal turned that gaze on me again, and I had to fight to not take a step back. This was the first time I'd been this close to him. He had an air about him that unsettled me. *Please don't let them see me sweating.*

"Parles català?"

"I'm afraid I only know a few phrases. My Spanish is only a little bit better, my apologies. I don't suppose any of you use American Sign Language? I'm quite fluent in that."

The men all chuckled, including Vidal, but the humor was gone after a moment.

"Bé." Ferrer said, clasping his hands in front of him. "We have gathered here tonight, a group of influential people in Catalunya. Our goal is to raise funds for the legal defense of our leaders who have been persecuted since Madrid took from us the ability to decide whether we want to have a referendum. Catalunya is one of the wealthiest states in all of España, and we are tired of carrying the rest of the country. We want to be in charge of our own destiny. I would think an American would understand that."

I swallowed and pretended I wasn't sweating like mad. "I can definitely see the appeal."

Ambròs Vidal frowned and directed that steely obsidian gaze on me. "There are people in this community who would punish those of us who speak out for independence. They are actively trying to take away our voice. I would caution you to take care who you listen to."

Paolo patted me on the shoulder again and I had to concentrate on not stumbling. Who I listened to? Had they been watching me? Did they know?

"Enough of this heavy stuff," Paolo said as if in warning to his friend. "Tonight we celebrate having a music teacher finally for our children, and we officially welcome you to our community."

I put on a brave smile. "Thank you. I appreciate it."

"Now, the rest of you go find the bar and tapas. I need to speak to Randall for a moment alone."

The other men left, with the exception of Jaume, who remained in the doorway.

"Vale. You are ready to play any of the songs? And you will accompany Pere?"

"Yes. I'm prepared."

"Molt bé. And to sing?"

I shrugged. "If you like."

He nodded again. "Wonderful. I had a question for you, though. When you put down the name Alonso on the RSVP, I thought perhaps it would be the gentleman in custodial services at Frederick Douglass. Do you know him?"

My mouth was a damn desert. "Our janitor Alonso? Not really. He doesn't speak English, and I haven't really been able to communicate well with him."

He stared at me for a long time. "What a coincidence, then, that you happen to bring another Alonso. Interesting."

"It is! I didn't know Alonso was such a common name here. I met *this* Alonso before I came to work at Frederick Douglass. I don't know him super well either, but we've been out a few times." I hoped that would derail his interrogation and get *my* Alonso off the hook. I hated that he wasn't here with me, but I was beginning to think it was good that he wasn't.

"Well, if you do happen to have a run-in with Alonso the custodian, ves amb compte. He is not who he says he is."

"Noted. I'll keep that in mind." *Shit.* I didn't know what else to say to that. "So, what time did you want to play?" I asked Paolo. Change of subject completely.

He looked at his watch. "I think we will still have guests coming in over the next hour, so how about we plan for eight forty-five?"

I'd been hoping to be out of there before then, but I should have known. "Whatever works for you."

"Vale. Let us go and mingle and hope your date has not run off."

What an odd thing to say.

"I'll follow you."

He told me to leave the guitar case in his den and then he walked me out to the large open-plan area that was half full of guests by this time.

"Let me get you a drink," Paolo said, walking me over to the bar. I accepted a glass of cava, figuring it would help calm my nerves a bit anyway, which was good, because Ruiz was nowhere to be seen.

"Actually, do you mind if I use the restroom?"

"It is right down that hallway," he said, pointing the opposite way from which we'd come.

I thanked him and walked with purpose but refused to scurry. I just needed a moment to collect myself and inspect the sweat damage. Once inside the room, I sloshed a bit of the cava on myself, cursed, and then I turned on the water with shaking hands and spoke directly into the top of the pin.

"I hope you can hear me, but Ruiz is gone. I don't know where he is. We are playing at eight forty-five, and then I will try to leave."

I dried my hands on a towel and put them on my stomach, trying to breathe through the nausea. The sweating was intense, leaving my suit feeling tight and scratchy, which heightened all of my anxiety to bordering on unbearable. I sat on the closed toilet lid and tried to slow my breathing.

I was on my own. I intended to get through this in one piece and the task force would hopefully get what they needed, but I wasn't going to worry about it. I just wanted to do my *job* job, not this clandestine shit. And I wanted *Alonso* Alonso. I was more worried about him than myself right now.

There was a tap on the bathroom window, and I jumped. It was frosted glass and I couldn't make out who was there, but I had a feeling...

I opened it a crack and heard the most wonderful sound.

"I'm here, amor. Cuida't."

"Are you okay? Did you hear Ferrer asking about you?"

I couldn't make out all of Alonso's face in the darkness outside the window, but just hearing his voice and knowing he was out there eased my fear. I hoped he was well hidden.

"Don't worry about me. Play and leave as quickly as you can."

I nodded, then touched the screen. "I'm so glad to see you."

He frowned, looked behind him, and then he was gone.

I washed my hands again and took a few deep breaths before I headed back out to the gathering. There were probably sixty or seventy people there, most of them older than me. I still hadn't seen Pere yet, so I approached Doriana.

"Hey, sorry to bother you, but have you seen my date? I seem to have misplaced him."

"Oh, I haven't," she said, but her smile seemed fake. "Please, come and meet some of the other parents from the school." I shook a few hands and then they all started to introduce themselves and ask me questions.

"Thank you, I'm enjoying working with the students at Frederick Douglass very much. Um, senyora Ferrer? I was hoping I could see Pere for a few moments?"

"Oh, yes. That would be good. Let me have Jaume show you to his room."

It seemed like Jaume was rarely very far from either Doriana or Paolo, and he certainly was an intimidating presence.

"This way," he said, and he led me up the staircase to the second floor of the grand home. The views of the ocean from the bank of windows both downstairs and along the staircase were stunning. I was sure they'd paid quite a premium for this property. I'd heard about this side of Castelldefels. Heard that even fútbol player Lionel Messi lived in this area. That didn't mean as much to me as it probably should have, but I'd smiled and acted impressed.

Pere's room was at the end of the hall on the opposite side of the house from where all the action was taking place. I knocked on the door and pushed it open carefully.

"Pere? It's senyor Sutter."

The boy was sitting on the floor and didn't look up from his book when he said, "Come in please."

He was dressed in a tiny suit, his hair gelled back from his face as he turned his big brown eyes on me.

"Wow, you look so handsome," I said as I knelt down next to him. "That's a nice suit."

"Thanks," he muttered. He stared down at a picture book, which I was sure was an old one as his reading level was way higher than that.

"You hiding out up here?"

He shook his head. "No. My stepmother said I had to stay in my room until it was time to play, that this wasn't a party for children. She also said she didn't want my suit to get messy."

"I already spilled cava on my suit coat so we can both be messy, how about that?"

I got my first genuine smile from him.

"Did you want to go through your piece together before we go out there?"

He shook his head. "Papa always says that if you don't know it before you go onstage, cramming in practice at the last minute isn't going to help."

"I suppose he's right." I sat back on my haunches. "Does your father have parties like this a lot?"

He let out a big sigh and his shoulders fell. "Sí. At least once a month. I'm never allowed to go. He says it's all boring adult stuff and that I wouldn't have any fun, but I would like to see what everyone is wearing. I like to look at the fancy clothes. I try to look through the window as they arrive."

I smiled at him. "It is pretty fun. Do you ever go to fashion shows? Or watch the red carpet before award shows on TV?"

He made a comical confused face and I laughed.

"Red carpet?"

"Yes, before the big awards shows, they lay out a red carpet at the entrance and all of the guests walk on it and get their pictures taken. Some of them get interviewed by reporters and they talk about who designed their dresses. It's pretty cool."

"Have you ever been on a red carpet?"

I smiled fondly, remembering my first time. "I have, in fact, a few times. But my first time was for the MTV Music Awards and everyone wore pretty silly things. It was very funny."

"What did you wear?"

"Ah," I laughed. *Nice, Randall. Sometimes you shouldn't mix your music career and teaching career.* I had to remember that some of my stories from rockstardom were not appropriate for kids.

"My band recreated the cover of one of our favorite albums." And that was all I was going to say. I didn't need him hunting down pictures of my band dressed like the guys on the cover of Muse's *Black Holes and Revelations* album. Those suits were awful. I'd gotten stuck with the gold lame that was obscenely tight and itchy as fuck. Rig kept blinding me every time the light hit the mirrors on his suit. Halo ripped his pants. It had been hell trying to perform dressed like that.

"I like fancy clothes," he said, and I figured I'd dodged a bullet. "I like to draw pictures of fancy clothes. Someday it would be fun to make them myself."

"That's wonderful. Do you know how to sew?" Oh, my heart. If Alonso had been here, I would have immediately made him agree to teach the little guy.

"I keep asking la meva àvia to teach me on her sewing machine but she's too busy with my cousins. I don't get to see her very often. She lives in Morocco."

"La meva àvia? I don't know this—"

"I think you say grandmother in English?"

"Oh. Thank you. I'm still figuring out Spanish as well as Catalan. It is quite confusing." I wanted to ask if this was his mother's family and assumed it might be. I bet he really missed his mother. Depending on what happened with this investigation, I would be sure to ask them to arrange for him to visit his mother.

"It's time," Jaume said from the doorway, and then he spoke Catalan to Pere, who went to the bathroom and washed his hands. He came back shaking them and stood beside me. He glowered at Jaume and shoved his hands in his pockets with gusto. Guess the kid didn't like the bodyguard either.

"Are you ready?" I asked him.

He nodded, resigned. I bet this was not how he wanted to play for his father, with a big crowd.

"Remember, whatever happens, we cover for each other. Always go back to the part you know and I'll be right there."

He gazed up at me with his big brown eyes and then

suddenly he grabbed my waist, hugging me tight. He was acting so brave, but his little body trembled as he squeezed.

"Hey," I said, finally tugging his arms free and kneeling down to his level. He stumbled a bit and caught himself by grabbing my coat. "Whoa. Hey, it's going to be great. You're playing so well. Know that all the people out there could only dream of playing like you do. You're going to be awesome."

He grinned at me, and then Jaume cleared his throat.

"Now."

I shot him a look of warning as I stood, taking Pere's hand. I don't care how big he was, I refused to let him intimidate me. I led my student past him and down the hallway to the staircase. As we rounded the bend on the steps, I heard Paolo quieting the guests. Doriana stood at the foot of the stairs and she smiled as she straightened Pere's tie.

"Make your papa proud," she said, kissing him on the cheek.

He stiffened, and I gave his hand a squeeze.

Paolo gave a long introduction in Catalan as we waited on the stairs and there were occasional shouts from the crowd.

I peeked around the corner of the foyer and saw Paolo giving a heated, dramatic speech. I wished desperately that I understood what he was saying. All I knew was it wasn't merely a, "Please, give what you can" kind of appeal. He punched his fist into his other palm and raised his hand in the air with a finger pointed. The crowd clapped for him and nodded approvingly. Then he said something and smiled and the rest of the room laughed with him.

"And now, my part of the bargain. I promised entertainment, and I always deliver, do I not?"

The applause went on for a long time.

"My beloved son Pere turned ten years old recently, can you believe it?"

More applause.

"He asked me if someday we could play together, and I told him he would have to practice really hard. Then, as if his wish was granted, our beloved escola Frederick Douglass finally hired a music teacher, who is himself quite an accomplished musician. You might have heard of his American rock and roll band MoonCraft." There was a round of applause and a few of the women cheered. "Join me in welcoming Randall Sutter, and my darling boy, Pere Josep Ferrer."

"Let's do this," I said, giving Pere a fist bump. Then I leaned down. "No matter what happens, I'm so proud of you."

His relieved smile had me ready to spit nails at his father.

"La guitarra," Jaume said as he handed me the guitar.

It was my turn to feel unsettled. What exactly were these people expecting from me? How was Ferrer going to play this? And where the hell was Ruiz?

Pere walked with his head high into the room and straight over to the white grand piano with an elevated bench that made it more accessible for him. There were two stools nearby, but I walked past them to stand where Pere could see me. I'd told him to pretend like it was just the two of us in the room, to try to ignore the others. He was doing a good job of that now.

I looked around and smiled to the crowd, giving a little bow. I looked for Ruiz, but he was still nowhere to be seen. While I tested the tuning on the guitar once more, Pere ran through a couple of scales and then linked his fingers in front of him to stretch out his hands. Just like I'd taught him. I loved this kid.

"And what will you be playing, senyor Pere?"

Pere looked to his father and said, "Per veure l'amor."

A sound of approval emanated from the crowd and they all applauded the choice. Apparently the song, which translated to "to see love" was one of Paolo Ferrer's most beloved songs.

"Well, I'll be a proud papa." Paolo patted his son on the

shoulder and then stepped back away from him. He gave me a curious smile and then nodded.

I waited for Pere to start and off we went.

He struggled with his pace the first few bars and then he ran with it. He was actually playing a bit faster than we had in practice, which meant I had to work to keep up with him. His little brow furrowed and he worried his lip, but the kid played beautifully, better than he had in school.

When he finished with a flourish, he looked to his father, his eyes full of worry—and it was Paolo who applauded the loudest. He reached for Pere and picked him up right off the bench and swung him around.

And I had a new fear.

Please do not let this man exploit this precious boy.

"Let's hear it for my wonderful boy!"

The applause continued, and he set Pere down to take a bow. Pere turned to me with a proud smile and gave a very grown-up bow to me.

"And let's hear it for our new music professor. Thank you, senyor Sutter, for honoring us with a classic piece of Catalan music. Very appropriate for this evening."

The crowd continued to applaud loudly. I smiled, waved a hand to be professional—and then I saw movement outside the windows. The floodlights glinted off the visors of police helmets.

I kept a strained smile on my face and concentrated on breathing evenly.

"And now, we all know that I am a bit of a competitive man," Paolo said as the room erupted in laughter. "So along with this wonderful performance with my son, I challenged Randall to play a few songs with me."

The crowd was audibly impressed and they continued to clap as we moved over to the stools, prepared our guitars to play, and waited for them to settle in. I hoped that whatever was going on outside, no one would get hurt, especially not Pere. All I could do was play and hope for the best.

"Would you like to choose the first song, Randall?"

"I would. Are we singing?"

"Sí, és clar. You start. We take turns."

Alrighty then.

I played the opening cords to "Light My Fire" as performed by Jose Feliciano, which had been fun to learn. I was a huge fan of The Doors and learned to play many of their songs when I was young, but this version was special.

I sang the first verse and we harmonized on the choruses. I kept the vocal pyrotechnics to a minimum at first, but by the end of the song, I was fired up, so to speak. I used the guitar as a percussive instrument as Paolo continued to strum and play an intricate solo. When it was over, the applause was the loudest yet, and Paolo reached out to shake my hand.

"You are quite good," he said in a low voice. "I'm very impressed, Randall." And he nodded as if to apologize for his previous attitude toward me. "You want to start the next one?"

"You go ahead," I said, and he went into "Malagueña." This one had been the most challenging song of the three to learn. I wasn't a hundred percent with the lyrics, so I let him sing it, watching him closely.

Paolo Ferrer was every bit the talented guitarist and vocalist he believed himself to be, which was a pleasant surprise. And the longer we played together, the more respect I saw in his gaze. If nothing else came out of this event, perhaps he'd at least go on to tell the other parents at the school that their teacher was indeed qualified to teach the kids.

We were about to launch into some Julio Iglesias when two things happened to derail our performance.

I caught sight of someone I hadn't expected to be there... with someone I wouldn't have imagined she'd be with.

Camille. On the arm of Ambròs Vidal.

She did not look happy to see me, or more fittingly, she didn't seem happy to be *seen*. She hadn't said anything about coming while we were shopping. Why was she with this guy who was many years her senior? And scary?

And second, there was a commotion at the back door and several big guys went running outside.

Paolo saw it too, and he held up a hand. "We're going to take a little break. Si us plau, eat and drink, my friends."

The crowd returned to loud chatter, oblivious to what was going on, and Paolo grabbed me by the arm.

"Come with me. Bring the guitar."

I let him lead me out of the room and into the office. He took the guitar from me and placed it in the case. "You should be more careful who you are dating, Randall."

I blanched. "Excuse me?"

"Your date is not who he says he is. He is Ejército de Tierra. Spanish Army. Did you know this?"

"I was told he was an art student." I wasn't lying exactly. I figured it would be safest to stick to our story.

"Yes, well, I believe he was here under false pretenses. Randall, my son adores you and that is why I invited you into my home, but there are matters at hand that don't involve you, and I fear you are being used."

That was not at all what I thought his reaction would be.

"My apologies if my date caused any issues. He seems to have abandoned me, so perhaps I should do a better job choosing in the future." My stomach clenched and I prayed once more to the sweat gods for mercy.

He glanced over my shoulder, and I turned to find Jaume standing behind me.

"He did not abandon—"

"I need to search your person."

I glared at the large man. *No fucking way.*

"Just as a precaution," Paolo said, attempting to placate me. "One cannot be too cautious."

No mercy from the gods. The sweat machine kicked back into high gear.

"Search me? For what?"

"We believe your date may have planted a listening device on you. Do you mind?"

Jaume reached for me, and I flinched at the same moment I heard a familiar voice in the hall.

"Randall! I had no idea you would be here."

Camille walked in with Vidal and came straight for me. She wrapped her arms around my waist and kissed my cheeks. I could tell by the overwhelming scent of eau de wine that she was feeling very good. "I'm sorry," she whispered.

Vidal pulled her away and spoke in her ear. She glared at him and then composed herself before turning to me with a small smile.

"You sounded wonderful, Randall. I'm sorry. I have to go."

"Thanks," I said to her back as Vidal practically dragged her from the room. What the hell was she doing with him?

I turned back to Paolo and started to say I needed to leave, when Jaume grabbed my shoulder.

"Take your hands off me," I said as I twisted away from him.

"Jaume," Paolo said, shaking his head. "My apologies, Randall. But remember what I said. Be careful who you trust."

I nodded to him. "Please tell Pere I'm so proud of him. He was so excited to play for you."

I gave Jaume a look that I hoped let him know I was annoyed and not scared shitless. I said good night and made my way toward the front door. All of the guests were leaving, speaking in hushed tones and looking rattled. I joined the flow of traffic headed out the door to find several soldiers in full uniform with big-ass guns, standing around taking note of everyone leaving the party. I made my way through the packed driveway and out to the street. I couldn't go the direction of the rendezvous without running into a large group of soldiers, so I went the other direction, figuring I would work my way through the neighborhood. There had to be another way to find them.

And I managed to get turned around.

Since I couldn't find the van, I wanted to at least get as far away from Paolo's house as possible. I kept walking into the darkness until I reached a quiet neighborhood with few lights on in the houses. It was after ten by this time, and my heart had finally slowed to a normal pace when a car came whizzing around the corner.

I recognized the Saab.

Alonso screeched to a halt and climbed halfway out of the car.

"Get in."

I hesitated. Paolo's words had shaken me. *They're using you.* In that split second before I decided I didn't care if it was the wrong move, my insecurity flared to life and I thought *maybe he really is that good of an actor. Maybe this is all a job to him.*

"Amor. Let me take you somewhere safe."

My only other option would be to try to find a cab in a neighborhood that was mostly empty and far from the city center.

"Okay." I walked around the car and got in the passenger side.

"Keep your head down," he said to me and he sped away. With his lights off.

THIRTEEN

I was sleepy but so wired from worrying all night that I was shivering in the front seat of Alonso's car. I had the seat all the way back so I could remain out of sight, as he had to drive close to the Ferrer house to get out of the neighborhood.

"Is everyone gone?"

"Nearly. Are you hurt?"

He reached over and tugged on the lapel of my suit coat. He pulled a small metal disc off of the fabric, rolled down the window with a hand crank, and tossed it out.

"What was that?"

"That was the listening device my comandante put on you. I had my own. Did anyone hurt you, Randall?"

"No," I said, surprised. "Jaume was going to search me, but then he got interrupted and Paolo stopped him so I was able to leave."

He opened his fingers, flexed them, and then tightened

them on the steering wheel. "I wish you would not have been put in that position."

"I needed to go. For Pere. What happened to Ruiz?"

"I don't know," he said. "They are still looking for him." He glanced at me. "He was taken out of the house and forced into a black SUV, driven by Vidal's bodyguard. The task force lost him. They are trying to track his phone, but no luck finding a signal as of yet."

"He *what?* They *kidnapped him?* Oh my God! He was just gone...I thought he'd left or was snooping or something. I never thought—"

My stomach bottomed out and bile crawled up the back of my throat. This situation was spiraling out of control.

Alonso reached for my hand and squeezed it as he shushed me.

"He is trained for this. We all know what can happen doing this work."

"God, Alonso, Paolo asked about you! Asked if I knew you. He—"

"He was not one of the men who assaulted my father, but Vidal was there."

"*Assaulted?* Alonso—"

"One of the men pushed him a few times and he pushed back. My father is not one to be walked over. It was enough to upset the delicate balance of his health."

"Your parents...your poor mother must have been so worried. I'm sorry, Alonso. I feel awful, but I'm glad you weren't inside with me. They talked about you—"

"I heard everything," he said. "The device in your boutonniere." He glanced down at me before taking a turn a little fast. "You did so good, Randall. I hate that you were there, but you did so good."

I was quiet for a moment. "Then you heard what he said to me. That I can't trust you."

"And?"

I'd gotten into the car with him. I would do it again. "I trust you."

Alonso nodded and his hands adjusted on the steering wheel.

"Camille was there. With Vidal."

Alonso frowned. "Did you know she knew him?"

"No. I had no idea."

Alonso's eyes were scanning the road in front of him. We'd been driving longer than it should have taken to get back to my apartment.

"Where are we going?" I didn't recognize where we were.

"To Felip's apartment. It is the safest place right now."

I blinked. "Alonso, what is happening?"

"I don't...I'm not sure. Someone gave my identity to Vidal and I'm worried it was my team leader. They didn't just see my picture on the wall at the winery. They went there to confront my father, to tell him his son was a traitor. They threatened him. Then I was taken off of the assignment, and my family was left with no protection."

"Alonso, I'm so sorry. You should be with your family—"

"Not without you." He glanced at me. "I have taken care of them for now."

I leaned closer to him, placing a hand on his arm. He glanced down at me and then touched my hair with such a gentle gesture, I nearly melted.

"Baby," I breathed.

"I know. Let me get you to Felip's. I need to hold you."

I wanted the same.

But when we arrived, he parked and sat.

"What's wrong?"

He flicked his chin, and I peered over the dashboard. There were two uniformed Guardia Civil standing on the street outside Felip's building.

"Maybe it's nothing, but I don't like it." He put the car in gear and pulled out onto the street, pulling his cap down. "Can you hang on a little longer? I will take you to my uncle's. He lives in California but keeps a flat here for when he and his wife come to visit, though they usually stay at the guesthouse at the winery."

"Do you have a key?"

He huffed out a laugh. "I handle security for all of my family. Including Fermín's properties, which is why I knew where all of his cameras were."

Alonso drove away from the city center and out toward the Mediterranean, going north instead of South, which was the way we'd come. I saw signs for Park Besós before he pulled into an underground parking garage. He found a visitor's spot and parked the car, muttering that he was going to have to leave his car behind in the garage, that it was too conspicuous.

I knew that literally none of this was my fault, but I couldn't help but feel guilty that Alonso was trying to take care of me in the middle of this chaos. His eyes were bloodshot with dark circles beneath them, and he hadn't shaved.

He got out of the car and came around to open my door. He held out a hand to help me from the car and I took it even though I was plenty capable. He pulled me into his arms and held me tight, burying his face in my neck.

"I promise I will sort this out," he said close to my ear. "Let's get some sleep and I promise in the morning, I will feed you."

"Hey," I said, putting a hand on his cheek. "Promise me *you* will rest? I'm not going to break, I swear. I'm worried about you."

He buried his face in my hair, and for a split second I worried about the great sweating event of earlier this evening.

"It's been ages since anyone other than my family has worried for me."

I relaxed for the first time that evening, and gave him a genuine smile. "Then I have to make up for lost time."

He took my hand, kissed the back of it, and then led me to the elevators. As the doors closed, I thought...*I believe him. I will operate on the assumption that he feels as he says—the same as I do—and I will take care of him this time.* Because acting or not, he'd helped me through a difficult time. More than once.

We took an elevator up to the eighth floor of the building. Alonso hadn't told me much about the place, but once we got off the elevator and I saw the gorgeous art deco light fixtures, the deep gold carpet, I had a feeling it was quite upscale.

When we got to the door of the apartment, Alonso tapped in a code on the keypad and the door opened to a slice of paradise.

"This is a...second home?"

Alonso laughed. "Sí. My uncle is quite eccentric. He may have been a hippie back in the day, but his wife came from a wealthy family and they had some good investments on top of his earnings from the winery." He held out a hand. "There is a restroom in the bedroom. I don't know if there are clothes, but you're welcome to whatever you can find. My uncle usually keeps some things here."

He headed to the kitchen and was pouring us glasses of water as I slipped into the bedroom.

This place was *swank* swank. In any other situation, I would have been in heaven to spend a night here with Alonso. I still would be once I could settle in. I desperately wanted a shower, but instead I kicked off my shoes and stripped down to my undershirt—grateful that my antiperspirant hadn't failed me—

left my pants on, washed my hands and face before returning to the great room.

"I found some food," he said, turning to me with a tray of salami and cheese and crackers. "Are you hungry? I decided we needed a snack." He set it down on the bar and we each took a stool. All I thought I could tolerate was the crackers, so I took a couple. The water did a lot to help perk me up and after eating in silence for a few moments, Alonso cleared his throat.

"When I got back from the hospital, I called my commanding officer and he simply said, 'You've been relieved of your duties on this assignment.' He said *his* commander would review my actions on the case and determine my future in the Army reserves." He shook his head. "I was ready to leave after this op, but this is not how I wanted to do it."

I covered his hand with mine. "You've given a lot of your life to the service. I can understand feeling let down."

Alonso took a deep breath. "If I were a betting man, I would bet that the comandante never intended to actually investigate anyone."

"He certainly didn't seem as concerned as you did about this event. Guess he was wrong."

Alonso shook his head. "Word had to come from somewhere of my identity. Our personal politics are not to interfere with our duty. This all began because there was chatter in an online forum that Ferrer and Vidal had been raising money for the defense funds, but there were also rumors that they had bribed some officials to protect those involved in the separatist movement. There was talk that they had politicians in Madrid on their payroll as well."

"That's serious. Do you think it's true?"

"The last twenty-four hours have me believing anything is possible. Someone revealed my identity, and that leads me to think there are individuals in the military involved as well. I hate that this has put my family in a bad position and you in danger." He looked down at the counter. "My father was so upset. He reminded me that he'd discouraged me from enlisting after my required service. I love my country, and I love Catalunya. I am torn between my duty and my heritage. I was doing my job to protect the children. And you."

I reached out and rubbed his back, and he hunched into my touch.

"I'm sorry you were dragged into this," he whispered. "I hope it doesn't ruin your ability to do your job."

I shook my head and stood from the stool. "I'm going to be fine. And so will you. So will your family. I have faith. Now come on, you need rest. And I need a shower."

He glanced up at me and despite his exhaustion, he gave me a small smile.

"You want some company?"

I woke early the next morning alone in the bed, but I smelled something delicious in the other room. I stretched out for a moment and sighed.

We'd both been too tired to do anything other than wash each other and fall asleep kissing. It was certainly how I'd love to spend all my future nights—sleeping naked with Alonso wrapped around me—but Alonso was in such a precarious situation, and who knew if Paolo and his associates would let me be after the events of the previous evening?

I heard Alonso speaking to someone so I sat up in bed, realizing we weren't alone even at this early hour. I looked around and recalled that I'd left my suit in the bathroom and I'd have to walk past the open door naked. But then I noticed a black robe laying across the foot of the bed. I wrapped myself up in it and crept toward the doorway.

Alonso sat on the couch with his brother Mateu and two men I didn't know. They were huddled around a laptop speaking in Catalan. I meant to sneak away before he noticed me, but the door hinge creaked the slightest and all four men looked up.

Alonso's bright smile gave me courage.

"Amor," he said, standing and holding out a hand. "Come meet everyone."

The men I didn't know laughed, and Mateu's eyes went wide.

I pulled the robe tighter and faked a brave smile as I crossed the great room, the plush carpet feeling wonderful under my bare feet. When I reached Alonso, he kissed my cheek and one of the men moved over to make room for me.

"The teacher?" Mateu said, his voice cracking. "Cecilia's friend? ¿Què està passant?"

Alonso wrapped his arm around me and squeezed my hip as we sat together.

"Ell és el meu xicot. And since he doesn't speak Catalan yet, anglès, si us plau."

Mateu opened and closed his mouth a few times. "*Boyfriend?* I'm sorry, Randall. I just—"

"Didn't know your brother was bi?" Alonso interrupted. "Now you know. May we continue?"

And that was that.

"Randall, this is Romeu and Leo, my mates from the Army. They were smart enough to avoid this current quagmire but they've offered to help me eliminate any remaining threats."

"Hello," I said, my cheeks heating under their appreciative stares.

"Molt de gust," Leo said, shaking my hand, followed by Romeu.

"*Very* nice to meet *you*," Romeu said, exaggerating his words.

Alonso rolled his eyes. "You promised to behave," he said to them, and they laughed.

"Randall? You know this woman?" Leo asked, bringing up a picture of Camille on the laptop.

"Yes, of course. Camille Durand. She works at Frederick Douglass with me. French and math teacher. What about her?"

"Her grandfather, Hugo Llucia from Andorra, is one of the biggest financial supporters of the largest Catalan separatist organization, GPI or Grup per la independencia de Catalunya. We believe she is the conduit between Ambròs Vidal and the funds from Llucia. We have intel that they are planning to meet up at the school during the holiday break to make some sort of exchange. Money for information. We need to be there. If we can get proof of this connection, then we can insist the task force take action, or we can turn over our intel to Guardia Civil and hope for the best outcome."

"How can I help?" I asked, knowing Alonso would not want me involved.

He surprised me by turning to me and taking my hands. "We were hoping you might be willing to visit their flat, your French friends. Perhaps you can take them their Christmas gifts or something before they leave for holiday. Find out if Camille is planning to stay or leave? See if she says anything to you about the party? If we can nail down a time they are planning to meet, we can alert Guardia Civil, make sure no one is at the school. We don't want anyone else to get hurt. That is all. I don't want you to have any further involvement. You've done too much already."

"Of course. I can't believe Camille is involved—"

"We don't know how deeply she is, or if she knows what they are planning, but we don't want to spook her either and have her tell Vidal or Llucia. We're not sure why they keep meeting up at the school. I've searched that place head to toe and haven't found anything out of the ordinary, but that doesn't mean there's not a more significant reason the school seems to be the center of this group of people. It's a place where they can meet with each other that gives them a commonality, where if they met someplace in the community it might raise suspicions."

Leo leaned forward with his elbows on his knees. "I know this all seems nebulous, but there are Catalan independence groups that are currently on the terrorist list with the government in Madrid. They have not gone to the violent lengths that ETA have—"

"ETA?"

"Basque separatists," Alonso said. "You are familiar with País Vasco in the north?"

"You mean, like Bilbao? We played there."

"Tensions were much higher years ago," Romeu continued. "The current prime minister has been able to gain the support of the separatist groups and there is an uneasy peace between them at the moment. There was a time when ETA was a threat to all of España. You can imagine that none of us want to see this dispute between Catalunya and Madrid become like that. But we know that Vidal has connections to some very high-level officials. If he is using his financial resources to affect the outcome of legislation, or the court cases against those incriminated in illegal activity, we must put a stop to this."

"I didn't know," I said. "I'm afraid I'm behind on my international politics."

Alonso squeezed my knee. "We forgive you, guiri."

I raised an eyebrow at his use of the pejorative word for tourist, but I loved seeing the return of playful Alonso. I wondered if I would see more of this side of him if, or when, this situation was resolved. Would we continue to see each other? I wanted that so much. I knew I shouldn't become used to having someone at my back like he'd been since we met, but that's the thing about finding the person you wanted to be *your* person. Once you did, you didn't want to be without them.

But then I'd also found other people I cared about deeply in this country. My colleagues at the school. Pere. I didn't want anything to happen to them either.

"What about Ferrer? Do you really think he's involved?"

Alonso frowned. "We don't know to what extent, and after he tried to warn you, I'm not convinced he knows what Vidal and Llucia have planned."

"Okay. When do we leave?"

"We will go back to Castelldefels after you've had a chance to eat and rest a bit more. Mateu brought breakfast, and Romeu and Leo brought us clothes and a car. I will drop you off and we will set up surveillance at the school and your complex. I spoke to Fermín, and he will alert us if anything happens before we arrive. I am hoping this ends soon."

"Me too," I said. I wanted everyone to be safe.

Alonso nodded but his gaze was unsure, as if he thought *I* might still be unsure.

"Was there any word on Ruiz?"

"They found him dazed and wandering the beach," Leo said, rolling his eyes. "He didn't know how he'd gotten there. Other than a headache, he seemed fine. They probably drugged him and questioned him. Here's hoping they weren't able to get any intel from him."

We ate breakfast and I spent the time watching Alonso and his mates talk about a mission they'd been involved with a few years prior, and his whole demeanor was different with them. He was at ease, laughing, comfortable. I noticed Mateu watching them as well with a frown. He got up to take his dishes to the kitchen and began cleaning up the takeout containers.

"Thank you for breakfast," I said as I stood next to him.

"Oh, de res. No problem, I mean."

I laughed. "I *am* picking up some Catalan. I know that one."

He frowned at his brother again and then looked back at me. "Can I ask where you two met? I do not mean to be rude, I'm just..."

"Surprised. He thought you would be. He actually rescued me during a protest near where he lives. He'd seen my band—"

"I remember. I was supposed to go with him, but I wasn't...I haven't been feeling up to socializing much. He tries to get me out, but the winery is my life right now."

"Right. I remember Cecilia saying you and Felip sort of swapped places, huh?"

He nodded. "I needed to be back here. It's better for me."

I recognized that waver in his voice. I thought perhaps this man, who was not much older than me, had been struggling. I could relate.

"Anyway, I didn't think I'd see him again, and then he showed up at my work, and then at the winery..."

"Ah, yes. Mama's birthday. I see. Well, I won't say anything. He should be the one to tell our family."

I laughed. "Don't want to be in the middle of that revelation?"

He shook his head and clicked his tongue against his teeth. "No way." Then he laughed. "Our family is wonderful, and they will be happy for him, for you both. But they are a lot to take. I hope you will see the former and put up with the latter."

I smiled at him. "I can handle it."

He nodded. "Good. Because I've never seen him look at anyone like he looks at you." He gave me a warm smile, patted my shoulder and then headed back to the couches.

And I exhaled.

. . .

The men left us a few minutes later and as soon as they were gone, Alonso took me back to bed.

"I know we don't have much time," he said, and that was all the encouragement I needed. I let the robe fall and he was out of his clothes with superhuman speed. I laughed as he backed me onto the bed. He spread my legs and pushed my thighs until my knees were at my shoulders.

"I want to taste you, amor." He ran his tongue down my crease and over my hole. I groaned loudly. I had never been good at asking for what I wanted, but Alonso never gave me the chance to lament that fact. He loved to love my body how I loved to be loved. And he loved me with gusto, licking and kissing my tender flesh until I was a quivering mess. Then he planted his fists on either side of my hips and took my straining cock down the back of his throat.

He moaned with his lips sealed around my shaft and it only took a few bobs of his head until I was completely undone. I came with a shout, hoping that a fancy place like this had thick enough walls to muffle my cries of pleasure.

He licked at my belly and then moaned as he rose to his knees between my thighs, rubbed his cock over mine, and gave himself a few quick strokes before he covered my cock and belly with his spend. I'd never seen anything hotter in my entire life. He was so incredibly beautiful, covered in sweat and cum, his hair a mess, his lips an even darker red than usual and swollen. His chest heaved with his breaths and he had to catch himself on my raised knees to remain upright.

I held my arms out to him and he collapsed on me with a chuckle. "I cannot explain to you how special this is," he said when he could speak. "To share so freely with someone. This is unusual for me. All of what we do together, Randall. " He pushed up to look into my eyes. "I haven't felt like this before."

"Me neither." I said, swallowing the lump in my throat.

"Given that, my feelings are all over the place." And I was trying really hard not to cry. It was like all of the events, all of my fears, all of it cascaded down upon me until I felt like I was caught in a riptide, about to be pulled under.

Alonso brushed my hair back. "I'm right here with you, amor. Feel." He took my hand and pressed it against his chest where his heart was beating wildly and held it there. "You have my heart."

"And you have mine," I said, wishing for the courage to use that stronger word that I knew would change everything between us. Would it be enough to make him want to keep me?

He let me hold him while his breathing slowed. I ran my hands over his back, wondering about his scars. I figured I could at least ask about my favorite one.

"I know you have had many adventures that you probably can't talk about, but can I ask about, you know, I thought it was a dimple on your chin this whole time, but it's a scar isn't it? How did you get it?"

He barked out a laugh and rolled over onto his back. He scrubbed his face with his hands. "I do have a dip there, but the scar made it much deeper. I was wrestling with Felip. He put my face through a window once."

"No! Oh my God, how awful!"

"It was not a bad fight or anything like that. We were being rough in the house, which Mama forbade us from ever doing. I did him dirty, you know what I mean, and when he could finally straighten up, he grabbed my neck and went to push me against the wall, but I turned and broke a pane on the back door with my face. My chin got it the worst, but I have one here, and here," he said, pointing to his eyebrow, which I hadn't noticed because it didn't interrupt the thick hair there, and the other spot was at his temple.

"This one is really big," I said, tracing it lightly. "You could have been really hurt."

"Sí. Felip got in a lot of trouble for that. He didn't even rat me out for starting it."

"I never fought physically with my brothers. They pushed me around when I was little, then they just ignored me. I didn't have that fight-back reflex," I laughed.

"Because you are a lover, not a fighter," he said, kissing me with lots of tongue. Oh, he tasted so good. I wished we could hide out in this place forever, but just as I thought it, I worried about Camille and my friends.

As if he read my mind, Alonso's relaxed face tensed up. "I hate to leave here..."

"But we need to, I know." I drank in the sight of his naked body one more time, committing it to memory as much as possible. Whatever happened, I'd be writing a multitude of songs about this man. You could bet on that.

FOURTEEN

We were quiet on the drive back to Castelldefels, but he held my hand every moment he could. I didn't know which of us was grounding the other more. I wished we had his car, as I longed to dive back into his cassette collection. I wondered what he'd grown up with, what his first music memories were, what concerts he'd been to... Would we have time to have those conversations?

He seemed preoccupied too, his eyes darting around as he navigated the silver BMW Romeu and Leo had brought for him down C-31 out of Barcelona. I knew he'd gotten some sleep because I'd watched him for a long time the night before. He twitched a lot when he was sleeping, though, so who knew how restful it actually was for him. He was alert, his body tense. When he exited onto the city streets a few blocks away from my apartment, he squeezed my hand.

"I'm not sure if they installed any listening devices in your apartment before they left, but I don't have the scanner any longer. Since I've been relieved of duty on this mission, I'm lacking a lot of things I wish I wasn't, but I do have this," he said, reaching into the breast pocket of his flannel shirt and producing a white and silver disk. "It's not very hi-tech, but it will do."

"An AirTag?" I took it from him and turned it over in my hands.

"Sí. Please keep it on you, in your shoe perhaps. And I will give you a cell phone. They have probably cloned yours."

Now I was the one on edge. Throughout all of this, I'd known I was part of an intelligence-gathering mission, however I had been a tool, not the focus of the investigation.

"You think they're going to be watching me?"

He shrugged. "Either the task force or Vidal's people. It is possible. But know that I will be near, and Romeu and Leo. As soon as this meeting happens, we will hopefully have the information we need and this will all be over."

I had to ask. "And then what?"

He glanced at me, his eyebrows raised. "You will be able to go to work without fear."

I looked out the window and sighed. That's it? That was it.

He took my hand again, and I turned to him as he kissed it, leveling his deep brown-eyed gaze on me. "And I would very much like to spend whatever time we can together."

And I could breathe again. I smiled at him, my lip quivering a bit. I'd needed to hear that.

My smile fell as soon as we turned the corner to my complex and the driveway was blocked by la policía.

"Oh God," I breathed, and Alonso released his grip on my thigh.

He cursed and looked down at his phone. "Missed calls from Fermín. *Hostia.* He called before we left Barcelona and I didn't see it. Here," he said, handing me a cell phone. "I need you to listen to me, amor. It's charged, my number is programmed in. I can't go in with you. I'm afraid this starts now. Text me or call me, but if you call, stand away from your apartment. ¿Me entiendes?"

"Yes, yes. I'm just... Okay. I can do this. Promise me you'll be safe?"

He gave me the sweetest smile with a hint of "you silly man" to it.

"És clar. Of course, my love. You too. If you are in danger, I will be there. Rom and Leo also. I'm sorry to have to leave you. Tens el meu cor, Randall." He leaned over and kissed me and tears stung my eyes.

"And you have my heart."

I took a deep breath before sliding the phone into the interior pocket of my suit coat and slipping the AirTag in my left derby shoe. I opened the car door and climbed out, giving him one last look before closing it.

Alonso dropped me off on the corner and sped away. As I walked toward the police car, a fully strapped cop stepped forward.

"No puedes entrar."

"I live here," I said, pointing to...God, my flat door was open and there were cops outside. But it wasn't the same uniforms as Alonso's task force.

"Parles català? Castellà?"

I gave him the so-so hand signal and he called for another officer, who happened to be with Fermín.

"Randall, I'm so sorry," Fermín said. "I called la policía as soon as I saw what was happening on the cameras. They are going through the footage—"

"Mon dieu, Randall!" Josette and Sasha came running up. "What is happening? Who are these people that came to your flat?" Josette asked.

The police officer held them back and they spoke rapidly to him in Spanish. My head was spinning.

"Mr. Sutter, we need you to tell us if anything is missing," the cop with Fermin said.

I nodded and he led the way while the other cop kept the girls back. I waved to them and I wondered...why wasn't Camille with them?

Inside, my flat was trashed. Even though I didn't have many things, there had been a couple of house plants that I'd picked out with Sasha, that were now crashed on the floor. Fermín had provided the basic furniture in the place, and now it was all torn up and shredded.

"Fermín, I'm so sorry—"

"No, Randall, I'm glad you were not here." He said in a low voice only I would hear, "I tried to call Alonso—"

"I know. He just dropped me off."

Fermín looked at me, puzzled, and then nodded.

I was questioned about where I'd been. I explained that I'd been asked to perform at a gathering at Paolo Ferrer's home and then I'd stayed overnight in Barcelona with a friend. I couldn't help it, I glanced at Fermín. What would he say about me seeing his cousin? I wanted Alonso to tell the family when he was good and ready, not have them find out like this. *If* he was good and ready.

"You have not been here since yesterday afternoon then?"

I shook my head.

"Bé. Senyor Segura, what time did the break-in occur?"

"Early this morning," he said. "About seven o'clock." It was now close to nine. "My tenants in number two-two-six alerted me that the door was open and senyor Sutter was gone."

"We usually go to brunch on Sundays," I murmured.

"Please, senyor. Can you look in the bedroom as well?"

I walked into the room and my stomach dropped. "My laptop is gone."

And it was like the band robbery all over again. Like before, I had everything backed up to the cloud, but I had original songs that I'd recorded over the years which were saved to the cloud that could be accessed if they hacked my system. If anyone got past my security, they'd have access to my most private thoughts and creations.

"Anything else?"

I shook my head. "I have nothing else."

I walked over and picked up my favorite cardigan, which lay in the middle of the bed sheets on the floor, and wrapped my arms around it. It was literally the only thing of value I had left in this world.

I was tired of people taking things from me.

My instruments, my band, my sense of security, my Alonso.

The phone Alonso gave me buzzed in my pocket.

You okay?

No, I wasn't. But instead of being afraid, I was livid.

They trashed the place. They took my laptop.

"Senyor Sutter, are you missing anything else?"

"No," I said to the officer.

"Bé. If you can please wait outside while we finish processing the scene?"

I nodded, hugged my sweater tighter, and strolled out the door. Josette and Sasha were waiting outside.

"We will help you clean it up," Sasha said. "I'm so sorry. Why do you think—"

"Where is Camille?" I asked.

The women looked at each other, and then Josette spoke.

"She went outside to yell at the people who came to your flat. And then she left with them."

"She *left* with them? Or they *took* her with them?"

Both of their eyes went wide as if they knew something, enough to frighten them.

"You need to tell the police." My phone buzzed and I pulled it out of my other pocket. I didn't recognize the number, but it was local.

"Hello?"

"Randall, it's Camille. You need to turn it over to them or they will kill Pere and me."

I put a call in to Alonso on the phone he gave me and turned Camille on speaker, hoping Alonso would hear enough.

"Turn what over?" I asked, holding the second phone as close to the first as I could without being obvious. The police officer was watching me. He moved toward another officer and they began speaking rapidly. I was running out of time.

Josette and Sasha's eyes went wide. They gestured with their eyes toward the police officer and I shook my head. I had to take the chance that Alonso and his friends could track me. I didn't know who to trust besides them.

"The key," she said, her voice cracking. "The one Pere gave you."

"I don't have a key. Where is Pere?"

"He said he put it in your suit pocket— No!" I heard her squeal and a scuffling on the other end of the phone.

"Senyor Sutter, if you want to see your friend and your student alive, you will come to the school and bring the key. Come alone. If the police come with you, we will kill them, and we will find you."

I didn't recognize the voice on the phone but the person had a thick Catalan accent.

"I will come. Please don't hurt anyone."

"Get here in ten minutes. You will be watched. If you call anyone, we will know, and we will kill them. You don't want their deaths on your hands. None of this had to happen, but you meddled. Come alone."

"Okay."

The call disconnected and I put both phones in my pocket, keeping the line on Alonso's phone open. As I reached into the front pocket of my suit coat, there it was. A small key on a simple key ring. I didn't pull it out.

"I have to go."

"Please be careful," Josette said. "What can we do?"

"Keep this for me?" I handed Josette my sweater. "If I don't come back," I said, "tell Lara what happened. In fact, call her now. She'll hopefully be able to help."

I took off at a dead run, which wasn't very fast, but I ran on a regular basis to keep my lungs strong enough to sing for three hours a night if necessary. I cut through a few back streets so if the police came after me, they might not find me as easily. I thought it would likely take me longer than ten minutes to get to the school, but I would do my best. I had to.

How had Pere snuck the key into my pocket? And what was he doing with something so valuable? Then I remembered he'd hugged me extra tight before we left his room the night of the party. He'd seemed worried, and I'd chalked it up to performing at the party, but what if he knew what was going on?

I ran the half mile to the school and slowed to a walk about a block ahead of time. There were three black SUVs in the parking lot. I took a chance and I spoke out loud, hoping Alonso could hear me.

"I'm at the school. I hope you're here. If anything happens..." Fuck, I wasn't going to tell him I loved him like this. I wasn't going to be dramatic when he needed me to brave, when Pere needed me to be strong for him. "I'll see you soon."

I took a deep breath and let it out slow, glad I wasn't completely winded. I walked along the bushes into the parking lot and noticed the back doors to the school were open. How the hell had they gotten in? Wasn't the building alarmed? Why weren't there police?

I entered the back doors and stopped inside. Gathered in the atrium were Vidal and his driver, and three other men I didn't recognize. Camille and Pere were on the floor with their hands and mouths taped.

"Thank you for coming, senyor Sutter," Vidal said in a cold voice. "If you would be so kind as to give us the key."

"Not until you let them go."

The men I didn't know pulled out guns and pointed them at Pere and Camille.

"We can kill you and take the key if you aren't willing to give it up, but then we will for sure have to kill them."

Camille looked pissed more than scared. Pere had been crying but was trying to be brave.

"Why did you even have to involve the school at all? Why put kids in danger?"

"Senyor Sutter, this is not like the action movies where the villain details his plans to the hero. This is a transaction, that is all."

I reached in the pocket of my suit coat and my fingers found the cool metal of the key.

"Please let them go," I breathed, my voice shaking. "How do I know you won't kill us all?"

"No one has to die, but we are running out of time. The key, *now*," he said, and I heard the click of the safety being removed from the gun pointed at Camille and Pere. Camille glared at the man, and I thought perhaps she'd finally realized that she was in way over her head.

I saw movement out of the corner of my eye and suddenly Alonso, Romeu and Leo appeared from the rear of the building. They moving in concert, approaching the gunmen from behind so swiftly they took us all by surprise. They attempted to disarm them, but there was a struggle, and I lost track of Alonso. I ducked behind a pillar as two shots went off, my heart thundering in my ears. Everything happened so fast...

I peeked out and saw Pere roll out of the way and under a bench. Vidal charged me and I backed up, tripping over a planter bed and nearly falling.

"The key!" he growled, squeezing my biceps. I tried to throw off his hold and run, but he was stronger despite having twenty years on me, and before I could get away, he had a grip on me I couldn't shake off. He pulled my left arm behind my back until I cried out and reached around to get his hand into my pocket. I tried to fight him off, but I felt something tear in my shoulder, leaving my left arm useless and driving me to my knees. When I was down, he hit me in the right ear and I fell to the ground, my temple smacking a bench on my way down, making my vision go spotty.

I kept my fingers tight around the key but he yanked and yanked, then finally stood—and stomped on my hand. I cried out and went limp, which meant he was able to pry my damaged fingers open and take the key.

Vidal ran off, and I tried to get up, but I couldn't put any weight on my left arm and my right hand wouldn't work. I was able to get to my knees in time to see him run down the hallway toward Camille's classroom, dragging Camille with him. I shouted her name just as a flood of uniformed men came in, guns pointed at Alonso and his friends, who had subdued the gunmen.

"No!" I called out as Alonso and the others went to their knees with their hands clasped behind their heads. No, they were getting it wrong! It was the others—

I tried to stand and my stomach heaved, bringing me to the floor. My head smacked the floor again and it was goodnight.

FIFTEEN

Nothing made sense. When I woke up in the hospital, Josette was there, and she told me what had happened, told me the whole tale. It was even more awful than I'd thought possible.

"Camille's grandfather got her the job at the school so she could make contact with and help Ambròs Vidal and his men. They were taking money from people through extortion, threatening to reveal their part in a coup they were plotting. Camille had money, names of officials, everything in a file in her classroom, all for Vidal and her grandfather. She is not the person I thought she was. How were we supposed to know her grandfather was a *terrorist?*" she whispered. "And how she could do anything with that man...Ambròs Vidal is a horrible person. His wife has disappeared, and their kids. Can you believe it?"

"So they were arrested?" I'd asked.

"Oui, as well as our custodian, Alonso. He was involved in it too."

I knew that wasn't true, but I didn't know if I was allowed to tell the truth. The last thing I'd seen was him with his hands on his head and it broke my heart to not be able to tell her everything.

"Pere?" I'd asked her then, too close to tears. I would never be able to get the look of terror on his face out of my mind.

"He's okay. He's safe. His father has been here to see you. He's brought doctors to see you."

My left arm was in a sling and my right hand was wrapped. They had me on so much pain medication I could barely feel my body.

I'd thought they'd taken everything from me. Then Vidal ruined me. The doctor's words floated through my head. *Ligament damage. Nerve damage. Surgery. Possible loss of function.*

"Randall, you are going to be okay," Josette said, but I'd turned my head, unsure I could take any more...anything.

Lara came to see me next, letting me know she'd spoken with Fermín and was making sure everything was repaired at my flat. She was so grateful to me for saving Pere, saving her school...

"And Alonso?" I asked her, hoping she might know something.

She shook her head. "The man from the task force said he'd been arrested and wouldn't tell me anything else. I'm sorry. I don't know what else I can do."

I nodded.

All I wanted to do was go home and go to bed until it was time to return to school, if I could. Lara had offered to go with me to the school before classes started in case I was too shaken up to handle being there. Traumatic experience and all that.

"Randall, if you need to speak to someone, I will make sure you have everything you need. You are our hero."

Cecilia called. Fermín let her and Felip know what

happened to me. She said she'd be on a flight as soon as her school was out that afternoon, but I told her not to come. Josette and Sasha had already said they would take care of me when I was out of the hospital.

"I'm coming to Spain anyway, so I'll be over there to give you a gentle hug. Felip needs to go. In addition to what happened to you, his brother is missing. No one has heard from him and the family is worried. He usually tells them when he's been deployed."

I didn't know if I could say anything, but I hated for the Seguras to be worried. *I* was worried. I had no idea if he was okay. I knew there had been people he'd said that he thought were compromised, that he didn't trust. Could he be in trouble for real? What if he was being held because he'd gone against orders to save me? What if he was hurt? If he hadn't surfaced by the time I got out of the hospital, I would tell...someone. At the very least I'd tell his family. Maybe Mr. Segura could do something as his parent. I was no one to him. He'd called me his boyfriend in front of his friends, but would that even matter?

"Senyor Sutter!"

As I hung up with Cecilia, Pere came running into my room. He started to hurl himself into my arms, but then he noticed the bandages and his eyes grew wide. He settled for putting a tentative hand on my lower leg.

"Hey little man," I said, trying to smile. I needed to push myself up a little, but I was stuck. I couldn't use either of my arms.

"No cansis al senyor Sutter, Pere. He needs to rest."

Paolo Ferrer came in without any of the swagger he'd had before. He stood next to the bed, struggling to make eye contact.

"We brought you those flowers. I picked them out myself," Pere said, pointing at a large vase full of gold-colored roses and assorted flowers.

"They are beautiful," I said. "The biggest bunch of them all. That was very sweet of you."

Paolo patted Pere's head. "Wait in the hallway for a moment, Pere, so I may speak with senyor Sutter."

Pere lost his smile and gazed at me with watery eyes. "Thank you for helping us," Pere said. "I am looking forward to going back to class. I have a new song picked out for us to learn."

I smiled at him, wishing I could ruffle his hair. I shifted in the bed, which sent a wave of pain through me. I tried not to let it show.

He waved to me and slunk out of the room.

"Senyor Sutter," Paolo started, his chin quivering. His eyes were red and glassy, his hair a little unkempt. "Randall...I owe you a huge debt—"

"It's okay—"

"Si us plau. Please, let me explain."

I waited for him to continue.

"I was born and raised in a small town outside of Barcelona. Catalunya is my home. I have watched us grow and expand, becoming an important part of all of España. My parents instilled in me the importance of preserving our language and culture, hence my love of music. I've been very successful, and I know the most important part of success is to give back to your community. It was in that vein that I agreed to help some local Catalans who wanted to support our jailed politicians. What Madrid did in twenty-seventeen was wrong and sentiment among the people in my circle is that more of us needed to step up and ensure that Catalunya remains autonomous and gains back what we have lost. No more can they take away from us."

He stopped speaking and took a couple of shaky breaths.

"When they approached me to gather a group of likeminded people in Castelldefels, to embark on a fundraising campaign, I was honored to help. Only, it turned into something ugly, and I am ashamed of my part in what happened, especially what happened to you."

"Senyor Ferrer—"

"I had no idea that...that this would become violent. I was so full of myself, so self-absorbed, I didn't see how it was affecting Pere. *He* was the one who discovered that Camille Durand was the go-between with the men here and her grandfather. Pere was in her classroom before school that day before the party. Vidal came to the door and Pere saw him give the key to Camille. He heard him tell her in French to keep it safe, that if it fell into the wrong hands, everyone in our group would be ruined. Vidal had been to my house on many occasions so Pere thought he meant me, too. Pere saw where she hid it in a jar on her desk, and at lunch, he snuck in there and grabbed it." Paolo rubbed his mouth. "The key was to a cabinet in her room. Vidal had hidden a file there with names of everyone who'd given money, all of the meetings... I had no idea what he had done with the money we raised, or that he was threatening people. Bribing officials with that money."

He rubbed at his eyes. "Pere thought if *he* took the key, if he hid it, then no one would get hurt. Pere trusted *you* above anyone, and that is why he put the key in your pocket. He didn't want me to get in trouble and he knew you would do the right thing."

"He's a smart kid." I couldn't believe it. With all of these scary things going on, a ten-year-old boy tried to save his father. How would all of this affect him in the long run? Lara needed to ensure that he received counseling as well.

"I would have never had these people in my home, never have gotten involved with their cause if I knew they planned to commit illegal acts, or violence in our community. I hope you believe me. That you can forgive me. I have a lot to answer for with the authorities, but I have agreed to cooperate. I will do anything for my son."

His gaze traveled over my injuries and his eyes filled with tears.

"I will also do everything in my power to make sure you are able to play again, Randall," he said in a low voice. "Music has been my passion for as long as I can remember, and I know from playing with you, and what you have done for my son, that it is for you as well." He swallowed hard and stood a little straighter. "I have brought in two very prestigious surgeons to consult on your case. They have agreed. I want you to see them. If you are comfortable, I want them to determine the best course of treatment. I want to do this for you. It is the least I can do to repay you for saving my son's life."

And then his tears fell.

"I cannot imagine my life without my son. When they came to the house and took him from me at gunpoint, I was desperate to get him back. He told me what you did, how brave you were. You, an americano, trying to protect my little boy and our community." He covered his mouth with his hand and took a few shaky breaths before whispering, "I owe you my life. It would mean nothing without him."

I believed him. Sometimes it took nearly losing everything to realize what you have. Fear was a huge motivator.

"I'm...I'm glad he's okay. He is a wonderful boy. I couldn't let them hurt him."

"Let me take care of you, Randall. Whatever it costs."

"Paolo, I have insurance. It's okay—"

"The care you need will cost extra. You need to have these surgeons evaluate your injuries, there will be physical therapy, I want to do this for you. I am more than capable. Please. I could not live with myself if you lost that part of you."

His last words finally cracked me wide open. I could lose

music. Sure, I could still sing, but if I couldn't play guitar? That would very likely sink me into a depression I couldn't come back from.

"All right," I whispered. "I'll see them."

He placed a hand on my right arm, gently, and squeezed. "Gràcies. Thank you, Randall."

I had to hand it to Ferrer. He delivered on his promise. The surgeons came to see me, came up with a plan, and I was whisked into surgery the next morning. Shoulder repaired, hand repaired, a great prognosis.

I spent a total of five days in the hospital, and when I was discharged, Josette and Sasha took me home to a clean apartment with new furniture, thanks to Fermín. The women made sure I had a stocked fridge and there were a few more feminine touches than I'd had before. I had a few days before beginning physical therapy, and all of my treatments were covered by the Ferrer family. They even arranged for a car to come fetch me and take me to my appointments.

I truly felt what it meant to have a community on my side. Despite nearly losing everything, I'd gained something I'd never felt I'd had before.

Cecilia called a few more times while I was in the hospital, sent flowers to the hospital, and then Felip brought her to see me a day after I got home. She got on well with my French Foreign Legion, which was down to two members now. Sasha told us she'd learned that Camille had been arrested for her part in what turned out to be an extensive extortion and bribery operation that involved members of the Catalan government as well as local police and even, allegedly, the military.

When Felip came back from talking to Fermín, he was

down. It had been over a week and no one had any idea where Alonso was. I made a decision right then.

"I need to tell you both something, and you'll probably be upset, but please know I was trying to respect Alonso's wishes."

They sat on my couch and I sat in my new recliner, which had been so helpful after my surgery as I couldn't lay flat for quite some time without pain.

"Alonso? How do you... You know something about my brother?" Felip's demeanor changed from sad to on the verge of anger, and I was glad Cecilia was there to ground him with a touch to his arm.

"The night before I called you back in November, Cecilia, I met Alonso. He rescued me, actually, from a protest on Las Ramblas."

Cecilia and Felip exchanged looks. "That place is bad luck," Cecilia muttered.

"Or maybe good? Depending on how you look at it?" Felip covered her hand with his and smiled before turning back to me with a frown.

"We, um..." God, this was embarrassing. "He took me to his place and I stayed the night with him."

Felip looked on with interest, nodding for me to continue... as if he hadn't realized what I'd said.

"Okay," I said with a laugh, because Cecilia totally got it. Her eyes lit up and she smiled wide. I worried for a minute about whether there might still be a listening device in my place, but they deserved answers, and if someone was listening, maybe it would trigger a response and we'd find out where he was. "So then, Cecilia, you hooked me up with Lara, I got hired, and on my first day I fell off my bike...and Alonso rescued me again, although he was in a custodian's uniform and he acted like he didn't know me, nor spoke any English."

Felip's frown grew more severe. "Custodian? What the...
Go on."

"For a few weeks he ignored me, and I thought I was losing
my mind, but then I went to the winery with you, and he finally
told me he was on an assignment. At my school."

His frown changed from confused to concerned. "Dime
màs. What happened then?"

I explained what I knew, that he was close to discovering
what was going on with the separatist group, then their father
was assaulted at the winery—which no one had told Felip about
apparently—and that he was relieved of duty. "I don't know
where he went from there, but I had to go to perform at Paolo
Ferrer's home, and it turned out it was supposed to be a
fundraiser to help the legal fund of the separatist leaders."

Felip cursed, and Cecilia raised her eyebrows at him.

"Please continue," he said, all signs of jovial Felip gone. He
was scowling, which made him look even more like Alonso. I
was worried how he would react to the rest of the tale.

I exhaled and tried to shift in the chair a bit. It was getting
close to time for my next pain medication. I felt better, but
everything still hurt.

"Randall?" Cecilia asked. "Can I get you anything?"

I shook my head. "Thanks. I still don't know everything that
went down at Ferrer's that night. I left, Alonso picked me up,
and we tried to go to his place, but it was being watched. He
took me to your uncle's place, and we spent the night together
there." Still no recognition from Felip. I wasn't going to come
right out and tell him I'd had the best sex of my life with his
brother.

"Anyway, he brought me back here the next morning, and
the police were there because someone had broken into my
apartment," which caused Cecilia to gasp. "One of the parents
from the school called, told me to come to the school, he had

kidnapped my friend Camille, or so I'd thought, and Mr. Ferrer's son. Alonso came and—"

I sucked in a breath, remembering my helplessness, stuck on the floor while the police arrested Alonso and his friends. "He and his friends saved us. But I don't know what happened to him from there. There were Guardia Civil and la policía there. I don't remember seeing the men from the task force, but Alonso said he didn't trust them after he was relieved of duty." I breathed in and winced as a sharp pain shot through my shoulder.

"Randall, you need to rest."

I shook my head. "Felip, I'm sorry. He planned to tell you all about us, but I don't know where he is or how to contact him."

Felip was nodding as I spoke—and then he suddenly stopped and leaned forward.

"Perdó, Randall. Did you say 'us'? What do you mean 'us'?"

I sighed, and Cecilia chuckled, then pressed her lips together.

"By 'us,' I mean I'm in love with your brother, Felip. And I'm pretty sure he feels the same about me, unless..." But I didn't even want to verbalize my worry for fear I might manifest it.

"In lo— Randall, my brother is not gay. I mean, he's never said he was, but he's never brought anyone home...I just assumed... *My brother is gay?*" He turned to Cecilia. "How is he *gay?*"

She placed a hand on his shoulder. "Do you need me to explain how it works?"

He rolled his eyes and grumbled something in Catalan, which made her laugh even harder.

Then he turned back to me and his expression was so pained. "How could I not know? I shared a room with him! We used to go out together. He never..."

"To be fair, Felip, he said he's bisexual."

"You were probably too busy with other things to notice, I'm sure," Cecilia said, and she cracked up even harder.

Felip glanced between us and his mouth flopped open and closed like a land-trapped fish.

"I can't believe it. I mean no offense, Randall. You are a very attractive man. It would not surprise me in the least that someone would want to be with you, but *Alonso?*"

"No offense taken?" I would have shrugged but I knew it would be excruciating. "I'm sure he would talk to you about it if he could. He...planned to." Which sobered the conversation, as we still didn't know where he was. The only thing that helped me not feel totally adrift was that he wasn't just avoiding me. *No one* had heard from him. He was missing. And I had no idea what to do.

Felip slapped his hands on his thighs. "I am counting on him explaining himself. I will find him. Thank you, Randall, for telling me all of this. I am deeply sorry for what has happened to you."

"God, me too," Cecilia said. "I feel responsible." She cut off my attempted interruption. "No, I know I couldn't have known what would happen at the school, but I just feel awful."

She fussed over me for a while after that. I let her wash my hair, finally. I'd been ready to have Josette take the clippers to it, but she'd refused. She'd rinsed it as best she could, but Cecilia was able to get me over to the sink and really get it clean. She brushed it out and braided it to keep it out of my way. Then she fed me like a baby. At least she made it fun with airplanes and hangars.

"You know, someday this may be the other way around and I'll have such fun messing with you."

"I wouldn't dream of any other outcome," she said laughing, but her affectionate smile meant everything to me. She was never like a mom. No, she was too young for that, but she was my mentor and confidante. Her being here made all of this a little easier.

Felip spent the whole time on the phone. Fermín came back down, and the two of them spoke in heated Catalan. I knew they were trying to figure out which of their contacts could help. An hour and several phone calls later, they were exasperated.

"No one has seen nor heard from him. La policía has no record of him. Our family attorney has not heard from him and no one can find any information with the courts. I phoned his commanding officer and he claims they are not at liberty to disclose any information." He pulled at his hair. "I'm ready to go to Madrid and force someone to give me answers. He can't just disappear. Not in this day and age."

Cecilia went to him and put an arm around his waist. "Come on, let's go for a walk, okay?"

He nodded and she waved to me. "We'll be back shortly," she said. It was good for them to go. Felip was ready to explode.

"So you and my cousin, huh?" Fermín asked. "I wondered why I'd seen his ancient car parked nearby. No one else drives those cars around here." Fermín laughed, but it was a tired sound, and there wasn't much humor behind it.

"I'm sorry about all of this, Fermín. I'd understand if you wanted me to move out."

"Nonsense," he said, coming to sit at the table with me. "You are with my cousin. And you are Cecilia's friend. You are family. We Seguras stick together." He patted my knee and sat back with a frown. "You know those fools tried to recruit me for their cause."

"Really? Ambròs Vidal?"

He nodded with a grunt. "They were trying to get as many business people in the area to join in, donate money toward the cause. I prefer to stay out of politics such as this. I'm not happy with Madrid either, but we have businesses to run, and tourism is extremely important to this area. If people see this as a place of unrest, they won't want to come here.

"You know, besides this complex and one closer to la platja, I own two hotels here in Castelldefels. I started with one, using the money I received from the winery—my father splits his share between his sons—and I have scraped together every penny to buy more properties. I wish my taxes went more toward the people and businesses here, but I understand how things work. I just want to continue hosting people from all over the world who come to visit our beautiful country. Vidal is a menace. I am proud my cousin was trying to stop him."

I smiled. "He wanted everyone to be safe."

He sniffed. "He always does. He installs security at all of my properties, the winery, he is a good man. Doesn't ask for anything in return. I am happy he found someone. I hope when he is found and this is all over, you will continue to make him happy."

"That's all I want."

My friends couldn't take care of me forever. After a week of babying, I called Josette and Sasha and told them to go home to France as they'd planned, to spend the rest of the holidays with their families. They came over and stocked my kitchen full of food before they left and made me promise to call them if anything happened.

But there was another call I needed to make.

Mom picked up after the first ring.

"Randall! Honey, how are you? I've been hoping you would call soon."

Guilt crashed over me but I needed to get through this. I thought about Alonso's words. It was time to apologize.

"I wanted to wish you all happy holidays."

"Thank you. Where are you? You sound funny."

I swallowed. "I'm in Spain, just outside of Barcelona. I'm working here now. I, uh, the band broke up, and so now I'm teaching music at an international school."

She was quiet for a few beats, and I heard my sister's voice.

"Your sister's listening, and you need to say hello to your brothers—wait, *the band broke up?* What are you doing in Spain?"

They spoke over each other, and then I heard them calling for my brothers. They put me on speakerphone, and I told them an abbreviated tale of robbery, romance, and the re-creation of Randall Sutter, leaving out the part about terrorists and the fact that I'd been broken and was now on the mend.

"I'm enjoying it, though, teaching music. Just like Cecilia always said I would."

"That sounds...well, it sounds like you're in a good place, honey," my mother said, and I had to suck in a breath before I passed out. I had no idea what I expected from this conversation, but it wasn't for my mom to just up and accept my new life like I'd told her I might have tea instead of coffee with breakfast.

"Thanks, Mom. Can I talk to Dad alone?"

"I'm here."

I heard shuffling noises and voices for a few seconds and then the line was silent.

"Dad?"

"Randall. It's good to hear from you."

"Dad, I wanted to say...I didn't want to... Things have been a little rough, but I'm good now. I...I said things before that—"

"Randall, we don't have to—"

"I said things that were disrespectful to you and everything you raised me to be. And when you come close to losing everything, you realize what really matters. You and Mom sacrificed a lot for me to get where I am today, and I just want you to know how much I appreciate you both. I'm sorry I let my frustrations get the better of me. I should have been honest instead of rude."

Dad grunted on the other end of the line, and I heard him clear his throat. "Holidays aren't the same without you here. Think we might see you?"

He wouldn't come out and apologize, nor would he express his feelings. But just like that, we'd moved on.

"Not...for a while, Dad. I can't travel right now. But as soon as I have time off from school, I'll come. And apologize in person."

"Good," he said. "I will too."

My eyes burned, and I didn't trust my ability to hold back the sob threatening to break free. "Dad, you don't have to—"

"Will you be bringing someone with you?"

"What? Will I—"

Dad chuckled. "I assumed there might be a *person* that influenced your move to another country on the other side of the world."

"You assume correct." Dad had always had a preternatural sense about the love lives of his children. Whatever our hearts' desired, whatever schemes we came up with, or tales we told to cover missed curfews...he always knew. "It's complicated, but I'd very much like for you to meet him."

"I'll look forward to it." He cleared his throat again. "Good of you to call. Here's your mother. Love you, son."

I listened as Mom chatted excitedly about Mark's baby on the way, Dustin's promotion, and Matt's latest hobby, dirt bike racing. Mayra cut in to tell me that she wanted to hear all about Spain because she and her girlfriends were planning to go to Europe over the summer, and did I think I'd still be there?

"I miss you," I whispered, my energy completely flagging. "I've gotta go."

They all said goodbye and while it had been a pretty chaotic conversation, it was a start.

I wished Alonso could have been there to hold my hand, and that thought made me finally give up and cry.

Physical therapy was hard, and the center was closed for a week over the holiday so I continued to do the exercises as best as I could at home. I was invited to dine with the Ferrers for Christmas, but I wasn't feeling up to company. Fermín came by once a day to see if I needed anything, and I thought he was probably checking to see if Alonso had resurfaced. No luck. It had been more than two weeks and nothing...no word.

There was nothing in the news either. I checked every day. Lara hadn't heard anything. Felip did go to Madrid, and came back to Barcelona furious. It all felt so hopeless. I didn't know how things worked in Spain. Could they make someone disappear, just like that?

I knew I was sulking but I was in shock, in pain, and afraid, and the only person who could make anything make sense to me was...missing.

By the time the winter holidays were over and it was time to get back to school, I had enough function in my left arm to get myself dressed. My right hand was still sore and I couldn't do anything weight bearing, but I could brush my teeth and hair. Sort of. I hadn't shaved, so the day before school started, Josette came over and helped me. She remarked that I'd lost weight and prodded me to explain why I was so sad. As if not being able to play guitar wasn't enough. But that's what I told her. I couldn't tell anyone else about Alonso.

I walked to school with her and Sasha the first day back. As we entered the building, my heart stopped when I heard the squeaky wheels of the custodian's cart. But when it came around the corner, an older gentleman was pushing it.

"Pedro!" Josette and Sasha ran up to the old man, gave him kisses on the cheeks. "Randall, come meet Pedro. He has been our custodian since we came to the school. He hurt his back and was out for some time. It's so good to see you," they said.

He smiled at me. "Mucho gusto."

"Molt de gust."

His eyes twinkled and he nodded. "Bé"

I'd spent my time off studying Catalan instead of staring at the walls. At least I could communicate a little better now. And if Alonso ever came back, well, he'd be proud.

I said adéu to them at my classroom and closed the door behind me to have a moment of quiet. I'd tried not to make a big deal about walking into the building and it wasn't as awful as I'd thought it would be. My classroom still felt like my safe place.

There were two items on my desk that I hadn't left there.

"Oh my God."

I ran over, ignoring the shoots of pain in my shoulder, less now but still present.

My acoustic guitar. It still had my sparkly rainbow sticker on the back and the scratches from when I'd fallen down a flight of stairs next to the stage with it after a particularly rowdy show. It had no strings on it and there was a chip in the wood, but it was mine. How did it get here?

And the other item? My original laptop.

How in the world?

When I opened the laptop, a piece of paper fluttered out. I picked it up with shaking hands.

Soon.

My heart gave another heavy thud and I looked around the room.

It was Alonso's writing.

He'd been here.

But wait...had he done this before he'd been arrested? When had he been here?

The door opened and my first student of the day came bouncing in with her flute.

"Bon dia, senyor Sutter."

And that was all the time I had to wonder about Alonso.

At the end of the day, I was exhausted. I'd had well-wishers come by every class period, at lunch, and several lingered after school. Parents brought me gifts, they said thank yous, they'd baked cookies and treats, more than even the whole staff could eat in a week.

Ferrer had arranged for the car to pick me up after school and take me to physical therapy, so when I finally managed to extricate myself, I trudged out to the parking lot, digging in my pocket for a pain pill and swallowing it down with my last bit of water. It was raining, so I had the hood of my raincoat pulled over my head. The driver stood next to the open door to the backseat with an umbrella, and I thanked him as I turned, lowered myself to the seat, and then pulled my legs into the car. He closed the door and got in, started the engine, and pulled out of the parking lot.

I rested my head against the seatback and closed my eyes. I inhaled a deep breath for the first time that day—and froze.

That combination of scents...

Then I noticed Jeff Buckley playing quietly through the speakers.

I looked into the driver's mirror and spotted those deep red lips quirked into a smile.

And the chin dimple.

"Alonso," I breathed. I leaned forward and put my hand on his shoulder, ignoring my pain. "Is it really you?"

"Sí, amor." He made a turn, and I couldn't stand it.

"Pull over! What? How? Why?"

"I will answer all of your whats, hows, and whys, but if we don't hurry, you will be late to your appointment, and I won't have you missing your treatment."

"Screw the appointment! Alonso!"

He smiled and put a hand over mine. "I would say it is good to see you, but you look terrible."

"Thanks, I kind of got broken."

His smile completely fell. "It killed me to see him hurt you."

I sat back a little. "You were trying to keep anyone from being shot. I understood. What happened?"

He shrugged a shoulder. "After I subdued the first man, I went for Vidal, but he got away from me. His man went after Pere and I couldn't allow the boy to be hurt. Before I could get to you, la policía was there, and I was arrested."

"But why?"

"Rom, Leo and I were not authorized to be there. We were not acting on behalf of the task force. We were, eh...vigilantes?"

"But—"

"We were taken to jail, and nothing happens quickly in Spain, especially not during the holidays. We sat for three days before our comandante's commanding officer got us out, and then we were put into military custody for disobeying orders."

"But—"

"And then he discovered that his subordinate, *our* comandante, was also acting against orders, and on and on. Debriefing after something like this takes a long time. I wasn't allowed to contact anyone, amor, or I would have let you know I was okay."

"And Romeu and Leo?"

"They are home now as well."

"Please tell me your family knows?"

"I saw them this morning, after I brought your things to the school."

"How did you—? I can't believe you found my guitar!"

He shrugged. "I know some people in Barcelona. The items showed up in a pawn shop. I picked them up. Oh, and my parents want us to come for dinner this weekend."

"Oh God."

He laughed. "And Felip gave me quite the tongue lashing."

"I'm sorry. I wouldn't have told him anything, but you'd disappeared, and everyone was so upset—"

"I'm glad you told them."

"I swear, I will keep your secrets from now on, but—"

"I will have no secrets. I have resigned my commission. From now on, it's winery business and private security for me. And taking care of my broken boyfriend."

Tears stung my eyes, and I tried to breath normally but I was in shock. "I was afraid I'd never see you again."

"So was I," he said, reaching around to squeeze my leg.

He pulled into the parking lot of the surgery center where I'd been receiving my treatments and he parked. He didn't move right away.

"Alonso? Are you all right?"

He sighed. "Mostly. I am angry I. I failed to protect you."

"Please get me out of this car so I can touch you."

"I will," he said, still not moving. "But first, Randall, I would understand if you did not want—"

"Get me out of this car *right now*, Alonso Segura, or I will—"

"Or you will what?" His eyes widened in the rearview mirror.

I growled, and that finally got him moving. He climbed out of the car and opened the back door wide. He stood before me looking fucking gorgeous in dark denim jeans, boots, and a black parka. "Can I help?"

"I can do it myself," I said. But it took what felt like forever to get to my feet. He kept reaching out for me, but I shook my head, wanting to do it alone. Since I'd been sitting down, everything had tightened up, and I needed to move slowly. The pain pill had kicked in but my stomach was off. I should have eaten something with it. Too late now.

When I was finally standing before him, I tried not to slouch. My therapist had been all over me to watch my posture, otherwise my shoulder wouldn't heal right and I'd have pain for the rest of my life and on and on. Getting yelled at in Catalan when I barely understood was not fun.

Alonso sucked in a breath and ran a gentle hand over my right shoulder, glancing down at my bandaged hand.

"El meu pobre amor."

"Shush," I said. "Just hold me."

He approached me carefully, sliding his hands around my waist, holding me gently as he pressed a kiss to my neck.

"Tighter," I begged him. "Don't let me go. I won't break."

"But you *did* break," he whispered.

"I didn't *break* break."

"You did *break* break. I missed you so much, Randall."

I smiled for the first time since I'd passed out on the floor of the school's atrium.

"I missed you more. I mean, look at me. I couldn't even feed myself."

He pulled back and cradled my face. "This should have never happened. I'm so sorry. Please let me make it up to you."

Still smiling like a loon, I tapped a finger against my lip. "Take me to my appointment and then tell me I did a good job when my therapist, the evil Marta, tells me I'm not doing my exercises enough, I need to stand up straight—"

"Es la verdad. Sí. I plan to take you home and care for you as long as you need me."

I licked my lips and dragged my teeth over the bottom one as I smiled slyly. "I never *won't* need you, though, baby. Fes-me un petó."

That got me the full Alonso smile. He finally gripped my hips tight like I wanted him to, pulling me flush against him as he leaned in, his lips hovering over mine.

"Molt be, amor."

Stay Tuned for More...

If you liked *Under His Sheets*, check out the additional books in the Accidentally Undercover series!

In Accidentally Undercover, everyday heroes risk life and limb for the people they love, even if they hardly know their real identities. Join six amazing authors for six amazing new LGBTQ+ stories full of suspense, mystery, action, and happily ever after.

Check out the complete series on Amazon!
My Book

Author's Note

I first visited Spain in 2001 and fell head-over-heels with the beautiful and fascinating country. We visited Madrid, Toledo, Granada, and Barcelona, and I was completely smitten with the language, culture, and history. There was not a lot of food variety in the places we went (I still hold one cannot live on jamón y queso alone), there was not much English spoken, especially on the trains, and the Madrid airport felt like one you'd find in a dystopian novel. It all added to the adventure for me and I dreamed of returning someday, perhaps for an extended stay, to really work on my Castellano (Castilian Spanish) and have the experience of living in such an old, yet vibrant place.

Fast-forward to 2018 and my high-school-aged daughter had the opportunity to go on a school trip through EF Tours. I was acquainted with her teacher, Zoya, who has since become a beloved dear friend and tomfoolery partner, and she let me know that there were several of her friends and other non-school-affiliated adults going on the trip, so I told my daughter (she forgave me eventually) that if she was going, we'd all be going, because at that price, it was something we could afford for all of us, and she didn't get to have all the fun. Mom of the year haha.

This trip brought me to an entirely new Spain, as there had been many changes to the country I'd fallen in love with seventeen years earlier. There was a new level of diversity in things like food, shops, and advertisements from international companies that made Madrid, especially, feel much more cosmopolitan, like what I believed a large European city would be like. We visited Madrid, Toledo, Segovia, Burgos, Bilbao, San Sebastián, Saint-Jean-de-Luz in France, Pamplona, Zaragoza, and we ended our trip in Barcelona.

We happened to arrive in Catalonia during a time of political turmoil in the autonomous territory after the Catalan government had attempted to hold a referendum to determine whether or not the people of Catalonia wanted to vote on becoming independent from Spain. I'd had no idea such sentiments existed, though I was somewhat familiar with the history of conflict in the Basque country, which was much more tumultuous. It seemed wild to me, at the time, that a country so old would be having these movements for independence, so I asked a lot of questions when we got to Barcelona, especially when I started to see different flags flown from balconies. We did run into a few protests while we were there, but our guides kept us clear of them. We had a fantastic tour guide in Kolja and our local guides were so knowledgeable and patient with my many questions.

Being a history geek and long-time student of Spanish/Castellano, I absorbed as much about the history, culture, and language as I could from every stop of our tour, and when I returned home, I wrote a contemporary romance novel called *A Match Made in Spain* inspired by our adventure. I pitched it, I got some interest from a trad publisher, and then I was told they loved the story the way it was written, but if they were going to acquire it, it would need a lot of changes, mainly removing most of the cast of the characters. With this particular book, I was not interested in overhauling the story, so I self-published the book in 2021.

A year or so later, I decided to dip my toes in the audiobook ocean. With the help of narrator Jennifer Aquino, I found The Audio Flow, who hired Catalan narrator Carlos Reig-Plaza and the wonderful Torian Brackett to round out the cast, and my little book was brought to life. I loved the finished product so much and had been flirting with the idea of writing more books about the characters.

Then last fall, I received a message from Layla Reyne asking if I wanted to join an accidental-spy-themed group writing project, and just like Ethan Hunt, I chose to accept the mission. (See what I did there?) Those ideas on the backburner flared to life in the guise of Alonso Segura, younger brother of *AMMS* hero Felip. He'd had a bit of a mysterious background in the book that included military service, and I knew he'd be perfect for this assignment.

The Catalan movement for independence still has strong

support from the Catalan people, but the pandemic, the fallout from Brexit, and the sentencing of Catalan leaders to lengthy prison terms for their part in the failed referendum of 2017 dealt a serious blow to its momentum. In the summer of 2023, Spanish Prime Minister Pedro Sanchez began speaking of amnesty for the jailed leaders of the movement, which angered many Spaniards, and protests became violent toward the end of 2023. All of these developments led me to wonder, what would happen if a down-on-his-luck American musician was dropped into the middle of this maelstrom?

There you have it, the inspiration for *Under His Sheets*.

As for the "hijinks" I mentioned in the Language Note at the beginning of the book, I want to make something very clear. The movement for independence in Catalonia is a serious issue which I did not intend to represent lightly. Through Randall's eyes, you will see the arguments of both sides and the very real implications the people in Catalonia face as they determine their future. My intention was not to pick sides, but to respectfully represent a very real conundrum for the Spanish people. I watched various documentaries, read many articles, and though I took liberties and fictionalized some of the events, I attempted to present a realistic experience for the characters in the story. I see a lot of parallels between the conflicts we are experiencing currently in the United States, and that made for a lot of relatable moments. Most Americans are not aware of the recent political history of Spain, so I hope reading this fictional romance novel will encourage readers to do their own follow-up research.

Thank you for choosing to read *Under His Sheets: Accidentally Undercover*. If afterward you want more Spanish adventures, you can pick up *A Match Made in Spain* in ebook, print, and audio! I don't think I'm quite done with the Segura family, so *stay tuned...*

ACCIDENTALLY UNDERCOVER

Read the complete Accidentally Undercover series!

Under Her Roof by Allison Temple

Under The Gun by Cari Z

Under His Sheets by RL Merrill

Under The Table by Layla Reyne

Under His Name by MA Grant

Under the Radar by Linden Bell

ACKNOWLEDGMENTS

I'm so grateful to Layla and Alli for inviting me to join this adventure! I've become a bit of a romantic suspense junkie, and writing this book was like putting on a comfortable set of... Kevlar? I'm not done playing in this subgenre sandbox and I have these two awesome authors to blame/thank! And I'm so glad to be sharing this mission with Linden Bell, Cari Z, and M.A. Grant as well.

Mr. Ro has been wonderfully patient with me as I attempt to take advantage of my empty nest (well, with Velma it's not an empty nest), and I'm eternally grateful to him! I swear I'll get the dry cleaning picked up. And to my college kids, I love you and I'm so stinking proud of you.

To my assistant Rachel, you continue to be a rock goddess. Thank you.

Special thanks to Zoya and her endless network of folks! Berbex and Dzana thank you for chatting with me about life in International Schools. I appreciate you taking the time to discuss your experiences.

To Carlos, thank you so much for your patience with my endless questions (and terrible accent mark skills) and your candor. I appreciate your help in making this book the best— and most respectful—it can be.

Thanks to my writing communities sponsored by Rachael Herron and Jen Graybeal for providing the support I needed to meet my authory goals.

To my pals in BAQWA, thank you so much. And special

thanks to Vincent Meis for beta reading and giving such great feedback. Much appreciated.

Thank you to Phyllis Gerstenfeld for your feedback and also for embarking on this whole kids-in-college adventure with me. I appreciate you so much!

And as always, to the SBC. You lot are such a vital support network and I love you all dearly.

To my bestie, NLOD, I look forward to more adventures with you...

ABOUT THE AUTHOR

Whether she's writing contemporary romance featuring quirky and relatable characters or diving deep into the paranormal and supernatural to give readers a shiver, R.L. Merrill loves creating compelling, diverse, and inclusive stories that will stay with readers long after. Winner of the Kathryn Hayes "When Sparks Fly" Best Contemporary award for *Hurricane Reese*, Paranormal Romance Guild's Best Rockstar Romance for *You Can Do Magic*, and Daphne DuMaurier finalist for *Connection*, Ro spends every spare moment improving her writing craft and striving to find that perfect balance between real-life and happily ever after. You can find her connecting with readers on social media, advocating for America's youth, cruising around town with Great Dane Velma, cuddling with twin black cat familiars Frankenstein and Dracula, or headbanging at a rock show near her home in the San Francisco Bay Area! Stay Tuned for more...

Newsletter: www.rlmerrillauthor.com

facebook.com/rlmerrillauthor

instagram.com/rlmerrillauthor

tiktok.com/rlmerrillauthor1342

bookbub.com/profile/r-l-merrill

OTHER BOOKS BY R.L. MERRILL

Haunted Series: (Contemporary Romance)

Haunted

Fated

Bated

Jaded – (Coming Soon)

Minded Series: (Paranormal Spinoff of Haunted Series)

Minded

Blossomed

Father F'in' Christmas

A Peculiar Prom Night

Magic and Mayhem Universe: (Funny Paranormal Romance in the universe created by Robyn Peterman)

Shifted

Ghoul Me Once

Gator Me Twice

Magic and Mayhem/Shifted Collection

Fang Me Three Times

Fangtastic Four

Five Fanger Witch Punch

Hollywood Rock 'n' Romance Trilogy: (Contemporary Romance)

Teacher

Teacher: Act Two

Teacher: The Final Act

Contemporary Romance Series:

The Rock Season

Road Trip

You Fell First

The Heart Knows (Re-Releasing Soon)

A Match Made in Spain

LGBTQ Romance

Pinups and Puppies (Originally in Love Is All Vol. 2)

I Want, More – Bolder Breed Studios #1 (Originally in Love Is All Vol. 3)

Love and Pride – Bolder Breed Studios #2 (Originally in Love Is All Vol. 4)

Everything's Better With You: An MM Sports Romance

All I Wanna Do — Bolder Breed Studios #3 (Email Ro for your copy)

Road To Rocktoberfest 2024 (Coming Soon)

The Banes of Lake's Crossing (Historical Horror Romance)

The Fourth Man (The Banes of Lake's Crossing) (Historical Horror Romance)

The Redemption of Nathaniel Bane

The Absolution of Jonah Bane

The Gifted Series: (Supernatural Suspense/Paranormal Romance)

Healer

(Horror)

Exchange (Renewal) (Science Fiction)

Tap-Tap-Tap (Impact) (Horror)

Human Sacrifice (Innovation) (Horror)

The Sitter (Clarity) (Horror)

Joy Is A Phone Call Away – A More Perfect Union (Lesbian
Contemporary Romance)

The House Must Fall – Haunts and Hellions from HorrorAddicts.net
Press – May 2021 (Horror)

A Kept Woman – BAQWA Presents: Horror Show 2021 (Lesbian
Horror Romance)

Gods of Rock 'n' Roll (Free on Wattpad)

How Bittersweet is Karma? Free on Wattpad)

Let Me Stand Next To Your Fire (Queer Cheer)

Midnight in the Renaissance Elevator

Holiday Romance

A Peace Offering (Re-release)

Love and Pride – Bolder Breed Studios #2

Once Upon A Holiday Story 2024 (Coming Soon)

Audiobooks

The Rock Season (Kiss App)

Brains and Brawn (Kiss App)

Teacher (Kiss App)

Hurricane Reese (Kiss App)

A Match Made in Spain (Audible)

Healer: Gifted Book One (Audible)

Under His Sheets (Audible Coming Soon)

Non-Fiction

Horror Addicts Guide To Life Volume 2 - Edited by Emerian Rich

Death's Garden Revisited - Edited by Loren Rhoads (Out Fall 2022)